Rhiannon Lassiter wrote her first novel, *Hex*, when she was seventeen. She was born and brought up in London but now lives in Oxford with two small cats who sit on her manuscripts. *Hex: Shadows* is her second novel.

Reviews of *Hex*:

'A pacy sci-fi adventure thriller, both engrossingly written and confidently plotted . . . this is a considerable debut from a young writer from whom there will be much to look forward to.'
Books for Keeps

'*Hex* shows a considerable narrative style and a real flair for atmosphere.'
Philip Pullman, *The Guardian*

'A convincing, pacy story.'
The Independent

'A riveting first novel . . . a compulsive page-turning narrative complete with shoot-'em-up finale and a satisfying resolution.'
Michael Thorn, *TES*

Books by Rhiannon Lassiter

Hex
Hex: Shadows
Hex: Ghosts

Rhiannon Lassiter

MACMILLAN CHILDREN'S BOOKS

First published 1999 by Macmillan Children's Books

This edition published 2000 by Macmillan Children's Books
a division of Macmillan Publishers Limited
25 Eccleston Place, London SW1W 9NF
Basingstoke and Oxford
www.macmillan.com

Associated companies throughout the world

ISBN 0 330 37166 5

3 5 7 9 8 6 4 2

A CIP catalogue record for this book is available from
the British Library.

Typeset in Sabon by SX Composing DTP, Rayleigh, Essex
Printed and bound in Great Britain by Mackays of Chatham plc, Kent

Dedicated to all the Shadows
and to Ghost who shouldn't be left out.

Contents

Introduction

In the late 21st century, genetics experiments led to mutations in the population and the creation of a new breed of people known as Hexes. Feared for their ability to interface with technology, the Hexes were declared a threat to international security and across the world governments sanctioned their legalized extermination.

But the European Federation, the most tyrannical and repressive of the world governments, secretly authorized an illegal laboratory dedicated to performing experiments in the hope that the dangerous Hex abilities could be utilized or at least understood. In this facility thousands of children, unfortunate enough to possess the Hex gene, were experimented on, tortured and murdered.

In the year 2367 a Hex named Raven attempted to make the existence of this laboratory public, only to have it destroyed and the records hidden by agents of the British Government and the European Federation. But, despite the efforts of those same powers to locate and destroy Raven and her associates, the Hex group remains at large, and as long as they exist they are in danger.

1

Painted Honours

Alaric swung his flitter past the craft moving to intercept him and guided it into a spinning roll, setting a collision course for the bridge ahead. At the last minute he directed the vehicle upwards again and shot over the bridge, instead of into it, allowing the people crowding it to see the words emblazoned across the side of the flitter, proclaiming in brilliant gold: *Power to the People*.

As he guided his flitter around for another pass, avoiding the pursuing Security Services, Alaric glanced at the pandemonium below. The five skyscraper sections that formed the offices of the European Federation Consulate were surrounded by protesters. The bridges and archways that linked the Consulate to the rest of the level were blockaded by skimmers and pedestrians waving banners that carried the same slogan as Alaric's flitter. Portable holo units were mounted on the skimmers, projecting images on to the walls of the EF building. Other units, concealed among the protesters, created phantom images of flitters to distract the Seccies from their real targets. As protests went, it was a successful operation, but Alaric was aware that ultimately all their efforts would be useless. Already EF officials and Seccie operatives were pushing the crowd back from the doors of the Consulate and soon the demonstration would disintegrate.

Alaric was not under any illusions that this protest would change EF policy. It would be enough if news of the demonstration reached the public. Above the confusion flitters mounted with vid and holocams observed the scene, logos of the media networks painted prominently across the small aerial craft to distinguish them from the flitters of the demonstrators. The media was the real audience and Alaric was well aware of it. After passing low over the bridges he headed upwards to tumble past the news crews in a victory roll, displaying to advantage the words on his flitter. Next to the golden slogan was another logo, a red Celtic dragon coiled around a sceptre, the symbol of the most prominent political pressure group at the gathering. Alaric's group called themselves Anglecynn and would use any means from peaceful protests to terrorist attacks to expose the corruption and illegality at the heart of the European Federation. The dragon emblem was a warning to the watching masses that the EF could expect more than demonstrations if they disregarded the people who defied their control.

Even as he exhilarated in the thrill of the chase, Alaric longed to do some real damage, to hit the EF hard and fast and show that Anglecynn was a force to be reckoned with. But, despite their standing in the media, the group was too small to tackle the might of the European government on its own. Alaric knew his own limitations and, as he saw the Seccie operatives producing crowd control weapons down below, he knew that for the moment they had been reached. Clicking on his com unit he addressed the protesters in the other flitters:

'Time to pull back, people. They're bringing out the big guns.'

The five flitters swept away from the crowds and up

past the media crews. Taken by surprise, the Seccies were late in giving chase, and the little flitters took advantage of their delay to split up, each seeking a different path through the skyscraper maze of London to their rendezvous point in the depths of the city.

Several miles away and on a level somewhere in the middle of the city a black-clad figure turned away from the holoscreen with a derisive half-smile.

'Amateurs,' Raven said, without emotion. 'And naive at that.'

'Why naive?' Wraith asked. He had been watching the feature with the same fixed concentration he gave to all political reports but now he fixed his grey eyes on Raven, who had turned back to the mass of circuitry she had spread out over the blue-grey carpeting of the apartment.

'The machinery of political protest is defunct,' Raven replied, with a cynical expression, 'rendered obsolete by the microchip and the data pathways of the net.' She paused as she searched through a pile of tools for one she needed. 'This protest will vanish amid myriad media images, travelling faster than light through the information age. The records we released from Kalden's lab were discredited and eliminated within the week, the media nets moved on to new scandals and no one even blinked. You don't use the media by feeding it, but by controlling it.' She flicked a glance at the girl still sitting in front of the holoscreen. 'Ali should be able to tell you all about it.'

Ali Tarrell glanced up at the sound of her name and blushed as she registered what Raven had said. Ali's knowledge of the way the media worked was, at best, tenuous. The life she had had with her media mogul father had ended a year ago, vanishing even as she had become one of the invisible people, slipping between the cracks in the system and officially on record as exterminated for possession of the Hex abilities.

Ali turned back to watching the news, imitating Wraith. He found all forms of protest fascinating, as he still hoped that the Hexes could gain legal rights by taking their case to the European Federation which had issued the original law permitting their extermination. Raven was openly contemptuous of such a plan but Ali, coming from a more conventional and law-abiding background, favoured the idea. She still aimed to earn the respect of the ganger who had rescued her and her gaze lingered on his features, which could have been chiselled out of white marble, framed by equally white hair. The news report moved on to another story, losing Wraith's interest, and Ali looked away guiltily, glancing back over her shoulder to check that she had not been observed by the other occupants of the room.

Kez was nowhere to be seen and, to Ali's relief, Raven was again absorbed in her tangle of components. Although Raven was able to enter the virtual network that connected all computer facilities, she was as interested in the mechanics of machinery as in their datastreams. Ali wondered if that was why Raven seemed so much more able than her. Although Ali was two years older than the other girl, her abilities were much more limited. It was a fact that Raven never ceased to remind her of. Ever since their first meeting, Raven had exhibited contempt for someone she clearly regarded as an inferior imitation of herself.

Ali glared silently at Raven, whose long black hair fell over her face as she scrutinized the insides of the computer she was designing. It was particularly galling to recall that Raven was the kind of person that Ali would have despised during her old life on the right side of the law. Ensconced within a clique of popular pretty girls she would have felt safe to sneer at Raven, whose behaviour she considered to be almost psychotic. As if she could read her thoughts, the dark-haired girl looked up, her obsidian eyes meeting Ali's challengingly. Ali looked away again, not wanting a confrontation. The younger girl had been in a black mood for days, brought on by an argument with Wraith, which was lifting only now. Ali wouldn't have minded seeing them at odds, but the argument only served to remind her of the fact that, no matter how much they argued, they seemed determined to stay together. Ali had hoped Raven would take off someday but the possibility seemed remote. And Wraith, despite the fact that he condemned the apartment every day, showed no signs of intending to move elsewhere.

The apartment was not as luxurious as the one in the Belgravia Complex, where Ali had lived until six months ago. It was in a different area of the city and on a different level from her home. But it was desirable and expensive enough for Wraith to worry that they were unnecessarily exposed to the Seccies or the CPS. Raven wasn't worried about the Security Services; they had enough difficulty policing the ganglands without worrying about Hexes living secretly in the heights. But even she admitted that the CPS was a danger, if not to her, then to the others. They still had immense legal powers to kidnap and exterminate anyone with the Hex abilities. However she insisted they were better able to watch out for them here than in a place that they would have to defend against more conventional criminals.

Ali might admire Wraith but she was alarmed by the alternative he proposed. She didn't want to move down into the darkness of the ganglands any more than Raven did. However, her reluctance was motivated by fear and she suspected that Raven's was the result of pure stubbornness.

Just then the door to one of the bedrooms slid open and Kez entered. He had been a London streetrat before he joined up with Wraith and Raven. Since then he had changed enough for the brother and sister to trust him not to betray them. But Ali was still uncomfortable with the boy. Partly because of his gangland history and partly because Kez obviously admired Raven and she did nothing to discourage him. But the fact that Kez was able to take care of Revenge was an advantage to his presence as a member of the group.

Wraith and Raven's sister had never recovered from her stint in the CPS laboratories. As far as Ali could understand it, the eleven-year-old's brain had been directly linked up to a computer database with no experience in handling the dataflow. Most of the other children who had been experimented on in this way had been burned out, becoming mindless wrecks. But Revenge, who had possessed a greater potential to become a fully functional Hex, had survived the experience, though not unscarred. Most of the time she could function well enough to take care of herself, but her thoughts were so disengaged from her surroundings, scrambled as they were by the experimentation, that it wasn't safe to leave her on her own. Ali, Wraith, Kez and Luciel, the boy they had rescued from the CPS lab, divided the responsibility among them. Raven refused, considering the task a waste of her time. She spent hours in further research on the data she had stolen from the lab. From the questions she would occasionally ask them, Ali and Luciel suspected she was devising her own experiments to test the Hex abilities but she had said nothing to either of them and Wraith was too absorbed in his own project to notice. He was collecting information on the judicial process of turning people with the Hex gene into criminals, hoping to form a group of Hexes and their sympathizers who could work to challenge the extermination laws.

While Ali had been speculating on her companions Wraith had been thinking about what his sister had said. Turning away from the holoscreen, he crossed the room to sit on the arm of the chair next to her.

'How would *you* organize a protest, Raven?'

'I wouldn't,' she replied, not even deigning to look up.

'Why not?' Kez asked curiously, joining in the conversation.

'They serve no useful purpose,' Raven said. Putting down the tool she was working with, she looked up, her gaze shifting to include Ali as well as Wraith and Kez in her communication. When Raven chose to give her point of view, she always spoke to an audience. While Wraith often condemned her behaviour as reckless, he didn't deny that her judgements, when based on her own cynical philosophy of how the world worked, were rarely proved to be wrong.

'A protest is a public admission of incompetence,' Raven said coolly, shaking her hair out of her eyes. 'Its purpose is to draw attention to a situation in the hope of altering it. But, except in a few rare cases, the situation does not change because those who would care about the issue are either already alerted to it or, once they become aware of it, because they have seen the protest, believe that something is already being done. Demonstrations are just another form of media entertainment. They change nothing.'

‘The protesters against European Federation control don’t believe that,’ Wraith pointed out.

‘Naive,’ Raven shrugged. ‘As I said.’ Her expression turned wry as she continued: ‘But in any case, the anti-EF front doesn’t believe in the power of the people any more than I do. Did you notice that wasn’t the only symbol the flitters carried?’

‘There was a red dragon,’ Ali recalled. ‘The reporter said it was the insignia of a terrorist group.’

‘The group is called Anglecynn,’ Raven informed her. ‘They’ve been flooding the public nets with material for the past few years, combining information about EF corruption with threats of their next attacks.’ She gave a half-smile. ‘They’ve actually been quite effective at destruction of property, even a few attempted assassinations. They’re a small group, without much cohesion or strategy, but they might yet prove successful. The slogan on the flitter is not the real message, the dragon is. It reminds the EF that Anglecynn don’t just rely on media stunts to get their message across.’

The flitters cruised slowly through the darkness. After the chase through the high-rise levels and the tension travelling through the ganglands further down, the silence of the lower levels was almost soothing. The lights of Alaric’s flitter slid across the shadows, illuminating the debris that had built up around the roots of the massive skyscrapers. Centuries-old graffiti etched the ancient support struts with faded colours; light gleamed eerily back from the consumer graveyard beneath him; layers of obsolete luxuries sifted like sand into a rubble composed of the discards of the rich, long since scavenged and rejected by the poor and now abandoned like the roots of the city itself. The street-lighting had long since failed and the lights from the flitters pierced the darkness like a desecration.

The distant sounds that filtered down from above had gradually melted away and now the silence was complete. Alaric shivered and activated his comlink.

'Alaric to Jordan. My scanners show no signs of pursuit or surveillance. Do you concur?'

'*I concur*,' the girl's voice came back over the channel. '*No spooks or bugs. All scans are spangly and clean, now let's blow this joint and go home.*'

'Agreed,' Alaric replied drily and opened a new channel. 'Alaric to Dragon's Nest. My team is back and there's been no sign of a trace. Are we clear to come home?'

There was a buzz of static, punctuated by echoes from other signals before a voice replied briskly.

'*Our scanners agree there's no trace. Your team is cleared to approach, Alaric.*'

Alaric's hands moved swiftly over the control panel, speeding the flitter up as he signalled to the others that they were allowed to approach. Together they navigated the maze of support struts that rose from the sea of debris to become lost in the darkness above. The scenery passed by unchanging until the gloom was broken by a sprinkling of light in the distance ahead. The flitters slowed down as they approached a large plaza rising a little above the rubble and forming the forecourt to a skyscraper section which was not as damaged as the rest. Dim light shone from the windows as the flitters touched down on the cracked and pitted surface of the plaza and lit the way for the five newcomers to enter the building.

Alaric fell into step with one of his companions as they neared the door. Jordan glanced up at him, brushing her untidy brown hair out of her eyes, as he rested an arm over her shoulders.

'You did good work,' he told her.

'We all did good work,' she said, stopping to wrap her arms round his waist. 'But it's back to garbage city for all of us.'

Alaric frowned and rested his chin on the top of Jordan's head, drawing her into a hug so he wouldn't have to meet her serious blue-green eyes. The girl's voice was muffled as she continued:

'We all talk big, Alaric, but the EF knows we're not a serious threat. We're flies to them and they're just waiting for the right time to swat us out of the sky.'

'Then we'll have to convince them otherwise,' Alaric said firmly. But as he took Jordan's hand and led her into the building he wondered how that was ever going to be accomplished.

Anglecynn's headquarters were a safe refuge for the terrorist group. Far from the policed upper levels and ganglands alike, no one could find them in the depths of the city. They could expand through the abandoned buildings without fear of retribution and they had made the area their own. To Alaric and Jordan, Dragon's Nest was home and they relaxed as they entered its confines, secure in the knowledge that the proximity sensors would alert them to anyone approaching long before they neared the refuge. A short corridor leading from the entrance hall of the building took them to a large communal room. As Jordan headed for the battered Nutromac unit in the corner of the room, Alaric collapsed in an equally dilapidated chair and slung his feet up on the table in front of him. Heaving a deep sigh he stretched and sank back into the chair only to be jolted upright again by something landing hard in the centre of his chest.

It was a computer disk, and Alaric regarded it with confusion for a moment before its owner appeared in his field of vision.

'Got a job for you, Alaric,' Liz said, sitting on the side of the table.

Alaric groaned quietly. Like most of Anglecynn's so-called 'administrative' staff, Liz tended to disregard the work of the actual protesters. Unfortunately the group's efficiency depended on the information that Liz and others like her managed to dig out. Alaric could have pulled rank as a veteran of the group but instead he picked up the disk and looked questioningly at Liz.

'Information came through contacts yesterday,' she told him. 'Managed to filter through sources to us today. Comes from a sympathizer in the know – I thought you'd better take a look at it.'

Alaric had barely assimilated this brusque communication when Liz disappeared again and he was left looking quizzically at the disk as Jordan turned up with two cups of a thick black coffee substitute.

'Thanks,' he said absently, taking a sip of the acrid substance, and then got wearily to his feet.

'What's up?' Jordan asked, glancing at the disk Alaric still held.

'More work,' he told her. 'Hopefully shouldn't take too long. I'll join you in a while and we can grab some food, OK?'

''Kay,' Jordan replied, taking over the chair he'd vacated. 'Wake me up when you're ready.'

Alaric made a mock grimace at the sight of her relaxed figure, tousled her hair affectionately and went to find a computer unit and check the disk.

Although most of Anglecynn's real members lived in the city's depths, they had sympathizers and contacts in more exalted surroundings. The disk was marked as being a transmission from a Daniel Hammond, an Anglecynn sympathizer and the son of the recently appointed security minister. According to the appended file he had been approached by an Anglecynn contact and asked to find out what provisions were being made for the prevention of terrorism. This transmission was his response and as Alaric reviewed the file he found it increasingly odd, especially considering the amount of anti-EF activity.

Since appointment of Adam Hammond as Security Minister (4.10.2368) plans have been in progress for a new crackdown on terrorism, especially activities prejudicial to British relations with the European Federation. These plans have been superseded as of 3.1.2369 after a meeting between Adam Hammond MP (Security Minister and Head of the Security Services), Governor Charles Alverstead (Head of the CPS) and a Dr Kalden (unknown). Minutes of this meeting have been suppressed. The new security strategy is not focused on anti-EF terrorism. It is instead focused on supporting the CPS in their legalized extermination of mutants possessing the deformative Hex gene. The Security Services have pledged themselves to the elimination of all mutants within five years. Their efforts are concentrated on this one aim. Particular emphasis is being laid upon the capture of a mutant known as 'Raven' (described as a terrorist with the Hex gene). Transmission ends.

Alaric considered the transmission for some time, trying to understand all its implications. The increase in terrorist activity and the expansion of the ganglands had been the primary motivations behind the British Prime Minister's appointment of a new Security Minister. Now, if this information was correct, that Security Minister had decided to throw other considerations aside to support an organization that, because of its activities, had a politically unsavoury reputation. The combined threat of gangland crimes and terrorist attacks had been ignored in favour of apprehending a rogue mutant on the basis of a single meeting with the Head of the CPS and an unknown scientist. Alaric frowned at the screen. Other members of Anglecynn would rejoice in their good fortune in not being the focus of the Seccies' attention for a change. But Alaric found this new development too unusual to celebrate. Still frowning, he left the computer unit on and went to find Liz.

It took him some time to locate her in the rambling building. But he eventually tracked her down to a room several floors up where she and other Anglecynn members were watching a holovid projection of the raid on the EF Consulate. Crossing the room as unobtrusively as he could, Alaric came up behind Liz and touched her on the shoulder.

'Can I talk to you for a minute?' he asked.

Liz glanced up at him, looking slightly puzzled, then shrugged and followed him out of the room. Once they were in the corridor, Alaric kept walking, leading her back to the room where he had viewed the disk.

'That transmission you gave me,' he said. 'Have you had a look at it?'

'Yeah,' Liz nodded. 'Good news, if it's true. But it seemed a bit dodgy. Do you think it's a fake?'

'No, I don't think so.' Alaric thought for a second. 'At least if it is, it's very subtle.' He paused as they entered the room he had only recently vacated and guided Liz towards the computer unit. 'I want you to check something out for me.'

If Alaric had wanted to pay Liz back for preventing him from relaxing earlier, he would have been disappointed. Liz didn't raise a single objection as she slid into the chair in front of the keypad, waiting for further instructions.

'I want you to find out about the people mentioned in this document,' Alaric told her. 'Charles Alverstead, Dr Kalden, whoever he is, and this mutant, Raven. I want to know what's so important that the Seccies can't be bothered about tracking down an armed and dangerous terrorist group like us.'

Liz grinned but she was shaking her head as well.

'I'll do what I can,' she said. 'But I'm no hacker. I'll find out what's on the public databases, maybe a little more, but don't expect huge results.'

'Just do what you can,' Alaric reassured her. 'Any information would be better than nothing. Tomorrow I'll try and find out something more from this sympathizer: Daniel Hammond.'

Daniel was watching the news. His father had been pleased when Daniel joined him, finding his son's serious demeanour a welcome change from his daughter's levity. Caitlin was in her room sulking because the news interfered with watching one of the many amorphous programmes that dominated her life. But Adam Hammond had been firm. Not only did he insist that the news was a priority, today there would be an article of special interest to him, since the Security Services had provided it. Unknown to him, Daniel was watching for the same reason. His father's work had never been of much interest to him until Adam's elevation to Minister for Security.

Daniel's tenuous connection to Anglecynn had meant that his father's work had suddenly become more compelling, since it meant life or death to Daniel's associates. The transmission he had sent the day before, risking prosecution as a spy, was a reaffirmation of his commitment to the anti-EF front.

He didn't know what was going to be on the holovid this evening that so interested his father. But Adam rarely insisted on his right to watch the news, deeming it not worth Caitlin's complaints at being separated from the vid screen, so whatever it was must be important. However, article followed article without provoking any reaction from his father. The repeat of a feature on the attack on the EF Consulate drew a frown but that was already old news. Daniel shivered at the thought of what his father would do if he ever discovered his son's connections with the same demonstrators he condemned.

The feature came to an end and Adam leaned forward expectantly; Daniel focused on the screen as the next article began.

'In related news, the mutant terrorist with the illegal Hex gene, who was responsible for the destruction of a CPS facility causing the deaths of one hundred and thirty-seven men and women last year, is still on the loose. It is believed that the terrorist, who styles herself 'Raven', is hiding among the criminal element in the lower levels of the city. Today Adam Hammond, the Security Minister, said that information leading to her capture would be treated in the strictest confidentiality and he warned that citizens should beware of approaching Raven, who is probably armed and certainly dangerous. Nothing has been seen of Raven or the terrorists associated with her this year but last year her activities prompted a statement by the Prime Minister.'

The report cut to a segment of old footage showing the Prime Minister giving a statement to the House.

'. . . *The invasion of a CPS extermination facility, the fabrication of records from that facility, the publication of those records and eventual destruction of the facility concerned are all acts of astounding terrorism, perpetrated by a group of criminals sympathetic to the cause of illegal mutants. Rest assured these criminals will be caught . . .*'

The segment ended and the reporter continued:

'*Despite those assurances Raven has managed to elude the Security Services and is suspected to be planning acts of even greater atrocity. Political analysts cite this as an argument for greater EF control of Britain. The European Federation has the resources necessary to apprehend dangerous criminals of this kind without risk to those who capture them. But even without the aid of the Federation it seems the mutant plague will be finally brought to an end. Mr Hammond has pledged the Security Services to a widespread eradication programme, supporting the CPS in their mandate to rid this country of Hexes for ever. Britain will show the way by taking the first step and encouraging the rest of the world to do the same.*'

2

These Masks and Curtains

The vidscreen flickered in the darkened room, the recording frozen on the anonymous face of a news anchor. A pale hand moved against the moment control and the picture sprang to life again:

'*. . . seems the mutant plague will be finally brought to an end. Mr Hammond has pledged the Security Services to a widespread eradication programme, supporting the CPS in their mandate to rid this country of Hexes for ever. Britain will show the way by taking the first step and encouraging the rest of the world . . .*'

The screen blanked to black as the control twitched spasmodically in the hand of the watcher and for a while the room was dark.

The silence was broken by the sound of a door swishing open and light streamed into the room from the hallway, glinting off the red hair of the figure slumped in front of the vidscreen.

'Avalon?' a voice said, lifting a little in surprise. 'I'm sorry, I didn't think there was anyone here.'

'Don't worry about it,' the seated figure replied. 'Could you turn the lights on?'

'Certainly.' The newcomer turned gracefully and brushed his hand across a touch-sensitive panel set on the wall next to the door, causing soft lights to come on all over the room, illuminating the red and gold decoration that gleamed with luxury. 'What were you watching?' he asked, glancing at the control Avalon still held in her hand.

'A news bulletin I recorded yesterday,' Avalon replied, shifting up against the heavy red cushions to make room.

'May I ask why?' her companion asked politely, arranging himself carefully beside her.

Avalon shrugged in reply, then sighed and replied more explicitly.

'Looking for material, I guess. Seems the media are jazzed up on this terrorism story.'

'Is there an angle you want to use?'

'Maybe,' Avalon said slowly. 'A song with a terrorism theme, perhaps.'

'We could put ourselves on dangerous political ground,' was the response. 'Either we support the government in asking for more EF control or we glamorize terrorism. Perhaps something with ambiguous wording.' He paused to consider this and Avalon studied him thoughtfully. Cloud Estavisti cultivated a graceful poise that had catapulted him to fame as surely as his actual talent. He had an air of untouchability that shrouded him in mystique. Avalon liked to think that in two years of stardom she had learned something about media manipulation but compared to Cloud she was still a novice. From his streaked silver-blond hair and dark blue eyes to the holographic projections that floated in and out of sight around his plain white clothes, Cloud was not so much a human being as glamour personified and even Avalon was envious of such a quality.

Cloud came out of his reverie and raised his eyebrows at Avalon's intent stare. Gesturing towards the vidscreen he said:

'I came to see if you wanted to watch CultRock. They intend to show the new vid tonight.'

'OK.' Avalon passed Cloud the control and looked back at the screen as it came to life and flipped through a sequence of ephemeral images as Cloud searched for the right channel. With so many media feeds devoted solely to contemporary music, it took him a while to find it, but eventually the split-second images settled into a holographic projection of an alien city, spider-like creatures moving across the bridges and walkways to spin the buildings out of silk. The music itself made use of so many new effects that Avalon found it difficult to pick out the lyrics from the masking ultrasonics. Cloud set the image to project a metre out from the screen, not far enough to enclose them in the vid, and settled himself back next to Avalon.

Movement in the hallway alerted Avalon to the presence of more people and she turned to see the other members of what was loosely called her rock group clustering in to join them, drawn by the music pouring out from the custom-made speakers. Music was their life as much as hers and it never hurt to keep up on the competition.

'Isn't that Elohim's latest effort?' Lissa drawled, tossing her honey-coloured hair for Cloud's benefit as she slid into the seat next to him. 'Well, he's always been a little off the planet, but this time I don't think he's coming back.'

'Don't knock it, Liss, it sells,' pointed out Corin cynically.

'We sell,' Jesse corrected, sprawling sideways across an item of furniture designed for three people. 'And we don't have to get ethereal to do it.'

'Don't get complacent,' Corin told him. 'We could get

knocked off the top of the ratings just as quickly as Elohim.'

'Have you noticed how we are being emulated by groups with lesser talent?' Cloud interjected. 'Our style could easily cease being original and innovative and become last month's cliché.'

'It's all about style with you, isn't it?' Corin demanded belligerently. 'You're not a musician, so don't tell us how to work.'

The conversation continued argumentatively, band members jostling for position and cutting each other down. Avalon concentrated on the screen and tried to ignore it. They were always this nervous before an important exposure and they had all worked themselves to exhaustion on this new vid. Cloud was right. It was becoming harder and harder to buck the trends, with so many ready to imitate that their music was prevented from ever becoming truly distinctive. Recently they had been making more of the visual aspect, something in which Cloud excelled, to create a unique feel to their vids. But that wouldn't be enough without music to equal it and Avalon had been taking risks to achieve that. She couldn't explain how she did it, how she modified the electronic signals from her guitar to create sounds she knew the instrument should not be capable of, how she played with the equipment in the studio to create just the right sound. But she could put a name to the ability that allowed her to build a sound just this side of impossible and it was an ability that could get her killed, executed as summarily as every other Hex, despite the protecting shield of her fame.

Caitlin Hammond watched her brother with irritation as he shifted nervously in his chair. Daniel was always so jittery, she wouldn't be surprised if he had a secret girlfriend, what with all the hours and hours he spent on the vidcom. Usually Caitlin was too absorbed in her own affairs to pay even cursory attention to the fact of her brother's existence. But at the moment his fidgeting was irritating, distracting her from the vidscreen. She was about to suggest that Daniel went elsewhere when a soft chime indicated that there was someone at the apartment door.

'That's probably Zircarda,' Caitlin said with satisfaction, heading towards the door, knowing how much her brother disliked her friend. 'We're going to watch the premiere of the new Masque vid together.'

'Oh God,' Daniel groaned and hastily got out of his chair. 'I don't think I can cope with Zircarda Anthony at this time of night. I'll be in my room if anyone wants me.'

Caitlin answered the door as Daniel beat a hasty retreat, seeing that as usual Zircarda hadn't come alone. As the self-styled leader of the most popular clique in the Belgravia complex she considered it beneath her dignity to go anywhere without a couple of satellites. Currently she was accompanied by Mira, a long-standing clique member, and Roni, her latest protégée.

'Hi, Caitlin,' Zircarda said casually and she and Mira came inside, Roni trailing a few steps behind them. 'Has it started yet?'

'Not yet,' Caitlin replied. 'Come and sit down, the screen's already down.'

'Electric,' Zircarda said lazily, drifting over to the seat right in front of the screen and fiddling with the holo controls.

'Set it for room inclusive,' Mira suggested, heading towards the kitchen. 'I'm starving, Caitlin – have you got anything to eat?'

'Of course,' she replied and spent the next five minutes making drinks for the others while Mira rummaged around looking for food.

Having constructed herself a snack consisting of no calories whatsoever, Mira joined the rest of them in front of the screen.

'Isn't this the channel Ali's father set up last year?' she asked curiously and Caitlin flashed a glance at Zircarda, uncertain of how to react.

'Who's Ali?' Roni asked innocently and Zircarda made an expression of distaste.

'Mr Tarrell's daughter,' she said in a clipped tone of voice. 'She used to live here.'

'You must have heard of it, Roni,' Mira said more conversationally, interested in the sensation value of the story. 'It was a big scandal. She turned out be a Hex and the CPS came and took her away, right here in the Complex and everything.'

'And you knew her?' Roni was wide-eyed.

'She was a friend of ours,' Caitlin said sharply. 'And she can't have known what she was. Ali wasn't sneaky.'

'No, but what a way to find out.' Mira shook her head in disbelief. 'What a nightmare.'

'Well, it's over now,' Zircarda said firmly, taking control of the conversation again. 'Mira, did you manage to get tickets for the premiere of your mother's film?'

Daniel could still hear drawling voices through the closed door of his room and he turned on his sound system to drown it out. He was always amazed by the way the clique could drop people and never appear to think of them again. He vaguely remembered Ali Tarrell. She had seemed much like all the others, a pretty, if spoilt, teenager with too much money and no responsibilities.

But she was surely worth more than a minute's conversation, a year after her death, by people who had been her friends.

A shrill chirrup cut through the soothing waveform music emanating from Daniel's sound system, signalling that someone was attempting to contact his vidcom. Daniel silenced the music with a word and hurried over to sit in front of the com unit, touching the keypad to answer the signal. When he touched the control the screen remained black and Alaric frowned, wondering if there was a bug in the unit, until an obviously computer-altered voice spoke to him.

'Daniel Hammond?'

'Yes, that's me,' Daniel said nervously to whoever was watching him from the other side of the vidcom link.

'We got your message,' the voice continued.

'You're from Anglecynn?' Daniel asked and then clapped a hand over his mouth in alarm, realizing that if anyone was monitoring this signal he would have already condemned himself.

'Yes,' the stranger confirmed. 'There's no need for concern, this is a clean transmission.' Daniel wondered if he was imagining that a note of amusement had crept into the synthetic voice.

'What do you want?' Daniel asked. 'I can't talk to you here – it isn't safe.'

'Agreed,' the unknown terrorist replied. 'We want a face-to-face meet. You will be collected in one hour from bridge 9-75.'

'But . . .' Daniel protested and stopped as he saw the transmission had been cut. He tapped his fingers nervously on the side of the console for a minute before sending a new signal, this one to a public flitter firm. In seconds their operator had assured him that a flitter would be at his door in ten minutes to take him wherever he wished to go.

'And now it's time for what you've all been waiting for . . . the latest from Europe's most sensational rock combo: Masque. The new song's called "In the Dark" and showing for the first time anywhere CultRock brings you tonight the electric holovid . . .'

Ali's former friends would probably have been more horrified than gratified to know that halfway across the city she was watching the same channel that held them entranced. Although Ali had changed considerably since joining the renegades, some of her tastes were still those of the sheltered teenager she had been. Here, in a comfortably luxurious apartment, submerged in the images of a state-of-the-art holovid, Ali could imagine herself safe.

But safety was not the atmosphere Masque had sought to create with this video. Once it might not have touched Ali with its nightmare images; now it was a reminder of what lay beyond the haven of this room. The holovid showed dark passages leading ever downwards, a series of half-imagined horrors flitting from shadow to shadow, a world of terror realized by the shriek of a guitar. Ali shivered and then jumped as she caught sight of another shadow out of the corner of her eye. A soft laugh brought her back to reality.

'Raven!' she gasped, in mixed relief and embarrassment. 'I didn't see you there.'

Raven gave her a blank look, then turned back to the holoscreen.

'What is this?' she demanded.

'The group?' Ali asked, puzzled. 'Or the song?'

'Whatever,' Raven replied, with a touch of annoyance.

'It's Masque, their new vid: "Into the Dark",' Ali said nervously. 'Do you like it? I've got their latest lasdisc, if you want to borrow it.'

'OK,' Raven said, to Ali's surprise. Her dark eyes were distracted and she frowned at the vidscreen as if she was trying to remember something.

'Hang on, I'll go and get it,' Ali said and went to the room she had staked out as hers. It took her a few minutes to find the disc but when she got back she saw that Raven had not shifted position, she was still transfixed by the vidscreen.

'I didn't think you liked contemporary music,' Ali said. 'This latest disc is kind of freaky, though – their previous stuff wasn't like this.'

Halfway through what she was saying the final chords of the song signalled the end of the vid and the screen returned to the presenter's face. Raven blinked suddenly and turned away from the screen, her mouth twisted into a half-smile.

'The disc,' she demanded, holding out her hand for it.

'It's called "Transformations",' Ali explained. 'That's how come there's all the weird stuff on the holo. But there's a picture of the band on the other side.'

'Mmm,' Raven responded absently, flipping the disc case over to find it. Ali couldn't remember ever having seen the other girl less antagonistic.

'That's them,' she continued helpfully. 'The girl with the red hair's Avalon – she's the lead singer and guitarist – and that's Cloud and Corin, and Lissa, the sax-player, and the drummer's called Jesse.'

'Interesting,' said Raven thoughtfully. She seemed to look through Ali for a moment. 'Do you mind if I borrow this?'

'No, go ahead,' Ali managed to reply. She stared at

Raven, as the younger girl took the disc to her own room and disappeared inside, closing the door firmly behind her. 'Weird,' Ali said to herself and turned back to the vidscreen.

Kez soldered the last connection and looked critically at the mass of wires hanging out of the flitter's console.

'Hey, El, come and have a look at this!' he yelled and Luciel came round the side of the flitter to look through the open door.

'Are you done?' he asked.

'Yeah,' Kez said proudly. 'Custom job – nothing'll catch us when this thing's in the air.'

'Electric.' Luciel grinned and punched Kez's arm lightly. Of all the group he had changed the most in the past year. Since being rescued from the lab he had lost his scarecrow appearance and although his eyes were still haunted by memories of the experiments, he had managed to recover from withdrawal from the drug dependency the scientists had given him. He and Kez tended to spend most of their time together, although Luciel had managed to reconcile Kez and Ali enough for them to feel less uncomfortable with each other.

It was Kez who'd persuaded the gang that working for the Countess would be a good contact for them and he and Luciel accordingly spent hours working in the fixer's building in the heart of the ganglands, mending electronic equipment for a small fee. When there was nothing else for them to do, they worked on the flitter. Raven had given them the creds to buy it when Kez said he wanted to custom-rig one from the start. She dropped in occasionally, on her way to see the Countess, to give them advice and to give Luciel tools he had asked for. With Kez's practical and Luciel's theoretical science they were learning enough to make themselves useful to the Countess and get the flitter working the way they wanted it to.

'What's next?' Kez asked, looking over the console.

'Not much,' Luciel replied. 'I've got these power couplings linked up now. That just leaves the locks and the weapons system.'

'Yeah.' Kez frowned. 'Raven said she'd help us with that weeks ago.'

'I still can't believe it's possible.' Luciel shook his head. 'It *shouldn't* be possible. The power system she's designed for those laser weapons is the strangest thing I've ever seen. No one designs a system like that.'

'Except Raven,' Kez concluded. He sighed. 'I wish you could do the things she can, El. We wouldn't have to wait for her to be free.'

'She asks me and Ali questions all the time, to figure out what we can and can't do,' Luciel replied. 'She says she's working out a science of the Hex abilities.'

'She ought to be able to teach you something,' Kez insisted and Luciel shrugged. 'Come on,' he continued, 'we're done here for today. Let's go back to the apartment – perhaps Raven will have time to help us with the flitter tomorrow.'

Daniel wrapped his thick coat tightly around himself. The wind whistled through the towering skyrises and whipped across the deserted bridge. Greyness was all around him, the lights of the luxury heights were lost somewhere above him and the slums emblazoned with gang colours were invisible in the depths below. This was a no man's land, separating the rich from the poor, an area occupied only by transients, businesses and people on their way up or on their way down. The hired flitter that brought Daniel here had left ten minutes ago but there was still no sign of his contact. Shivering in the cold, he wondered what Anglecynn wanted with him. He had become a spy for the organization because he was ashamed of his father's connection with the brutal Security Services and he was afraid that greater EF control would be bad for the country. But he still hadn't fully committed to the movement; he lacked the courage of his convictions to break away from his father and the safe sheltered life he had in the Belgravia Complex and officially join Anglecynn. Thinking of the Belgravia Complex reminded him of his sister's conversation earlier; Ali Tarrell hadn't found herself safe there, despite her father's fame and riches. Perhaps he was fooling himself to think that he could support Anglecynn and not be in danger. Daniel shuddered and wondered if the time had come to leave home.

His musings were interrupted by the sound of a flitter swooshing past over his head and pivoting to land on the bridge beside him. The side window slid open to reveal a young man, not much older than a teenager, at the controls of the flitter. Dark eyes regarded him seriously before the stranger spoke.

'You must be Daniel.'

'That's right,' Daniel confirmed, nervously.

'Get in,' Alaric told him. 'It's not safe to talk here.'

Daniel hesitated for only a movement before crossing to the other side of the flitter as the door hissed open. It closed again behind him as he climbed in, and the flitter started to lift off as he was fastening his safety harness. The Anglecynn member sent the flitter weaving through the buildings and bridges with practised ease as he began to talk.

'We received your transmission,' he began. 'You said

that the Seccies were concentrating their efforts on helping the CPS.'

'Yes, it's true,' Daniel agreed, relieved that this was a question he could answer. 'Everyone's after the Hex sympathizers who destroyed an extermination facility last year.'

'I would have thought the Hexes were just about wiped out by now,' Alaric said thoughtfully. 'Why would they suddenly start attacking the CPS now?'

'I don't know.' Daniel shrugged. 'But the government seems to be taking it seriously.'

'And so should we,' Alaric added. 'If these Hexes have the Seccies this rattled, they might be useful to our cause. We need allies and the Hexes have suffered from EF control more than anyone else. I'm surprised no one in Anglecynn's thought of using them before.'

'No one really knows what Hexes do,' Daniel protested. 'They took a girl from my apartment complex last year but no one had even suspected she was a Hex. The CPS keeps all the details secret. All anyone knows is that Hexes are dangerous.'

'I'm suspicious of things that "everyone knows",' Alaric replied. 'And until I find out why Hexes are supposed to be so dangerous I think I'll give them the benefit of the doubt. In the meantime I'll need you to find out everything you can about this CPS operation and about this Hex called Raven. If we can contact her before the Seccies find her, we might be able to help each other.'

'I'll do my best,' Daniel agreed. 'But I'm not sure how long I can keep doing this. I think I'd rather work for Anglecynn directly than keep spying on my father. It seems dishonest.'

'I understand,' Alaric said quietly. 'The media brands

us as terrorists even though we're fighting for their freedom. Sometimes we have to sacrifice our consciences for what we believe in. But if you can get this information it would help immensely. After that, I'll see about finding you a place with us permanently.'

'Thank you,' Daniel said and meant it. The darkness of the ganglands where Anglecynn operated was no more frightening than the things he had heard since his father became the Security Minister. Some of the darkest crimes happened openly in the light and because they were legal no one protested. The Hex laws were an example of the kind of thing the law permitted: the legalized extermination of an entire group of people.

Luciel and Kez arrived back at the apartment to find it virtually deserted. Ali was sitting in front of the vidscreen in the main room; music pounding from behind Raven's closed door indicated where she might be; but there was no sign of Wraith or Revenge. Ali looked up and smiled as the boys entered and moved up so that they could sit down. Luciel came to sit next to her and Kez perched on one arm of the sofa, still uneasy around the former socialite.

'Hey, Ali, what's up?' Luciel asked. 'Have you been watching the vid all day?'

'Mostly,' Ali shrugged. 'There's not much for me to do around here. Wraith went out to get food, Raven's in her room, Rev— Rachel's asleep, I think.'

'You two should ask Raven about teaching you more of this Hex stuff,' Kez suggested. 'We could get the flitter finished faster that way and it would give you something to do, Ali.'

'I don't think Raven's really interested in teaching us,' Ali said quietly. 'As far as she's concerned she can do anything that needs doing faster and better than us anyway.'

'I still think you should ask her,' Kez persisted. 'If the two of you could do even half the stuff she can, we'd be so much safer. What's the point of being a Hex if you don't know how to be one?'

'A good point,' a voice said from the door and they looked round to see that Wraith had returned. The smell of Chinese food drifted across the room from the three bags Wraith was carrying, emblazoned with the holos of an expensive Chinese restaurant in the heights. 'Perhaps we should talk to Raven about it,' he continued. 'Do you think this will coax her out of her room?'

'I expect so,' Ali said smiling. 'She loves Chinese food and she's not really doing anything much. She borrowed one of my lasdiscs and she's been listening to it all evening.'

'Really?' Wraith looked surprised. 'What disc?' he asked.

'It's "Transformations",' Kez told him, having listened to the music seeping into the living room. 'The latest release by Masque.'

'Well, perhaps you can drag her away from it, Kez,' Wraith suggested. 'It's about time all of us talked.'

Kez nodded and headed for the door to Raven's room. He knocked loudly and was rewarded a few seconds later with it opening to reveal Raven dressed in her usual black, her hair a wild cloud around her face.

'Hi,' Kez said nervously, hoping she was in a good mood. 'Wraith got Chinese food from Hwang's. Do you want to come and eat with us?'

'Wraith went to Hwang's?' Raven smiled fleetingly and then glanced back into her room. 'Yes, I'll join you,' she said. 'Just give me a minute to finish in here.' Then she retreated, closing the door behind her.

As Kez went to tell the others Raven would be joining them he saw Wraith disappearing into Revenge's room but he doubted that she would come and eat with them. Revenge spent most of her time sleeping or endlessly playing computer games. She ate food from the Nutromac unit when they brought it to her and she let Wraith and Raven examine her but she rarely spoke to any of them and when she did her words didn't make much sense. Hoping that Wraith wouldn't be too disappointed with Revenge's progress, he went back to join the others. Ali had turned off the vidscreen and was unpacking the food while Luciel laid out plates on the long dining table. He heard the sounds of music cease from Raven's room and moments later she appeared just as Wraith came out of Revenge's room. His expression was bleak but he smiled when he saw Raven and she grinned at him.

'I see you bought dinner in the heights,' she said. 'To what do we owe the honour?'

'I thought it was time we all talked,' Wraith explained, coming to sit at the table. 'Did any of you see the news this evening?' The others shook their heads, Ali with a blush of embarrassment. She would have liked to say yes, but she rarely watched news programmes when Wraith wasn't around.

'So, what exciting news item did we miss?' Raven asked, heaping food onto her plate from one of the containers and passing it on to Luciel.

'The new Security Minister, Adam Hammond, has vowed to obliterate the Hex threat and has committed the Security Services to helping the CPS in exterminating Hexes,' Wraith said succinctly.

Ali went white and Luciel froze in the middle of helping

himself to food. Kez shot a look at Raven who, alone of them, still looked calm.

'Really?' she asked. 'Why the sudden crackdown?'

'Because of us,' Wraith said grimly. 'The government still claims we blew up the laboratory and they're calling us terrorists across the media.'

'I used to know Mr Hammond,' Ali said softly. 'He's Caitlin's father. I can't believe he's doing this.' Luciel reached out to squeeze her hand supportively.

'So we're notorious,' Raven said with a half-smile. 'What of it?'

'I think it's about time you taught Ali and Luciel how to use their abilities,' Wraith told her. 'And I think we should move down into the ganglands.'

Everyone turned to look at Raven, expecting her to protest, as she had so many times before, about leaving the luxury of their apartment. Instead she merely raised an eyebrow.

'All right,' she said calmly. 'It's probably time we moved and if we're going to recruit more Hexes, a training programme would be useful.'

The others stared at her in surprise. Kez was the first to speak.

'More Hexes?' he asked.

'Well, one more at least,' Raven replied. 'I discovered one today.'

'Who?' Wraith asked, meeting Raven's eyes seriously.

Raven smiled mischievously.

'A celebrity, no less,' she said. 'Avalon, the lead singer of Masque.'

3

Thy Known Secrecy

The Countess's building was unusually busy when Kez and Luciel arrived there the next day. The Countess herself was supervising operations as her guards loaded crates of equipment into two large flitters. Watching the activity with expressionless black eyes was Raven. Kez and Luciel looked at each other, then crossed the room to where the young Hex was sitting cross-legged on a crate marked *Explosives: Handle With Extreme Care*.

'What are you doing here?' Kez asked curiously as Raven looked up at him.

'Shopping,' Raven said briefly. 'If Wraith wants to move back into the ganglands we'll need some decent security. The Countess has a building she's not using about ten levels down from here, but the area isn't exactly safe. This stuff is to make it more secure.'

'How are you paying for all this?' Luciel asked incredulously and Raven shook her head with a grin.

'Hacked a bank this morning,' she replied simply.

Kez was about to ask what was in the crates when a familiar voice called out across the foyer:

'Hey, Raven, you ever wear anything that isn't black?'

Kez and Luciel turned round simultaneously to see two men in blue and gold gang colours approaching, their blue braided hair strung with gold beads.

'*You're* talking?' Raven asked, raising an eyebrow at their gang uniforms.

One of the gangers reached to ruffle Kez's hair and grinned down at him.

'Hey streetrat,' he greeted him. 'You still tagging along after this schizo?'

'Hey, Jeeva,' Kez replied, ducking out under the ganger's hand and aiming a mock punch at him. 'Blow up any buildings lately?'

'Can you believe it?' the ganger said, shaking his head. 'Half the Seccies are looking for us since that job and those double-dealing scientists blew the place up themselves.'

'Try getting the government to admit that,' Finn said scornfully and Kez nodded.

Finn and Jeeva had been members of the team that rescued Revenge and Luciel from the secret CPS laboratory last year, the raid in which the third member of their team had died. Kez was surprised to see them again, but relieved that they were no longer as antagonistic as the first time they'd met. The gangers seemed to have decided they could trust them.

'I hear you're setting up in ganglands,' Finn said. 'We're your escort into the depths.'

'Electric,' Raven said with a grin, jumping down off the crate. 'I think we're about ready to go.'

'Then let's fly,' Jeeva replied. 'Come and see the place we've got for you. It's not quite five-star accommodation, but I think you'll like it.'

'Can we come?' Luciel asked, looking hopefully at Raven.

'If you like,' she said with a shrug.

As Finn and Jeeva showed Raven the way to their flitter, Luciel and Kez tagging behind, Kez reflected on the difference between Raven and Wraith. Wraith considered the younger members of the group his responsibility and was often concerned for their safety, while Raven expected them to take care of themselves. Thinking over what he knew of the brother and sister he decided it was probably something to do with the fact that Wraith used to run with a gang, whereas Raven had grown up on her own. As Finn piloted the flitter out of the Countess's building, Kez wondered whether he preferred Wraith taking responsibility for them or Raven giving them complete independence.

Daniel caught himself glancing over his shoulder as he entered his father's study and shook himself quickly. Although he knew that no one could be watching him he still felt nervous. What he was about to do probably counted as treason as well as espionage and he couldn't help but feel guilty that he was betraying his father's trust. Trying not to think of his doubts, he headed for the computer terminal; Caitlin would be home from school soon and he couldn't afford to be caught logging into their father's private files.

As Security Minister, Adam Hammond had to work long hours both at his office in New Westminster and at home. As a result he had to keep a number of files relating to work on his home terminal. It was those files Daniel was looking for now. Although he wasn't a hacker, he had used his father's terminal before when his own wasn't sophisticated enough for research he needed to do for college. His father had given him access privileges, partly in the hope that Daniel would one day follow in his footsteps and work for the British Government. For a long time Daniel had known that was a forlorn hope; he could never work for the government as long as it was under the control of European Federation. But he had never told his father about his doubts and now that concealment worked to his advantage. Sitting in front of the terminal his fingers moved steadily across the keypad as he carried out his task for Anglecynn, searching his father's files for information on the CPS crackdown and on the Hex called Raven they were so determined to find.

Daniel soon discovered that Adam's files were encrypted, most of them using Ministry of Security passwords and code sequences. He copied those files to disk anyway, although he doubted that Anglecynn would be able to break the encryption. Then he started looking through his father's personal notes. They were also sealed with a password but it didn't take Daniel much thought to guess what it might be. Nervously he chewed on a strand of his loose brown hair as he typed in his mother's name:

> FRANCES <

The terminal began to decode the files and Daniel sighed. Ten years after his mother's death she was still helping him. Briefly he wondered what she would have thought of his involvement with the terrorists before shaking his head and returning to his work. His father's notes weren't detailed but they were informative and the most recent entries concerned the Hex threat.

> Arrangements for search for Hex named 'Raven': post rewards for information, greater surveillance ganglands, crackdown on hackers, regular 'stop and searches' by SS and CPS in lower levels. Also seek information on other terrorists' involvement in assault on CPS facility: male – white hair (Wraith); Irish male – green eyes, dyed blue hair; Caucasian youth – blond hair, brown eyes. Also seek information on missing test subjects: Luciel Liechtmann, Rachel Hollis and Alison Tarrell <

Daniel blinked and sat back, staring at the screen. As far as he was aware Ali Tarrell had been legally exterminated; his father's notes indicated differently. The term 'test subject' mystified him but the implication was clear: somewhere his sister's friend was still alive and possibly involved with the infamous Hex terrorists. Mechanically he set the terminal to copy these notes as his mind raced. The previous day he had been thinking about Ali and how her father's position hadn't protected her; now it seemed that even a vacant socialite of a schoolgirl had managed to look after herself and escape the all-seeing eye of the CPS. As he hid the disk copies in his jacket, Daniel suddenly felt hopeful again. If Ali Tarrell could escape and survive, so could he. Turning off his father's terminal and leaving the study, he tried not to think about the fact that Ali might not have survived at all.

Oblivious to Daniel's thoughts about her, Ali was feeling sorry for herself. Finally Raven had agreed to move into ganglands, which meant she would have to move there too. She had no choice but to stay with the gangers; she could never survive in the city on her own and succeed in evading the CPS. But moving into the lower levels meant that she would lose the last of her freedom. It wouldn't be safe to wander those levels on her own and she doubted that the others would give her anything useful to do. Day after day she would be trapped in the same place, a prisoner because of her own ineptitude. All the others could defend themselves and all the others had abilities they could use and trade, all except her and Revenge. She was as much a drain on the group as a brain-damaged cripple.

A tear slid slowly down Ali's face and she wiped it

away angrily. Just because the others thought she was useless didn't mean she had to be, she told herself firmly. Raven had said they would try to contact Avalon, the lead singer of Masque, soon. Maybe that was something she'd be able to do better than the others. As long as she could remember Ali had been meeting media celebrities; when they contacted Avalon she'd be able to understand the singer best and that would prove her usefulness. Biting her lip, Ali clung to the hope that through Avalon she'd find some way to prove herself.

The little flitter cruised slowly through the lower levels of the city as Finn pointed out the sights to Raven, informing her which gangs controlled the slums and who led them. The building the Countess had agreed to rent to them was in territory controlled by the Snakes, the gang that Finn and Jeeva ran with. As the flitter sank past broken bridges and derelict plazas, Kez and Luciel stared through the windows at the increasing proliferation of the blue and gold Snake emblem. When Finn finally set down the flitter it was on a slim archway connecting an abandoned plaza to an empty skyscraper section.

'This is it,' he told them, touching the door release so they could exit the craft. 'What do you think?'

Kez got out of the flitter and looked around. They were in the heart of gangland, the place he had grown up, and he felt his heart sink as he looked at the grime-covered walkways, the burnt-out lighting and the garbage strewn across the plaza. This was exactly what he had been trying to escape when he first met up with Wraith and Raven and now he had returned to it. Beside him, Luciel looked around curiously, his eyes round with wonder.

'It looks like nothing on earth,' he said softly.

Kez looked anxiously to see if Finn or Jeeva had

overheard, but the gangers were accompanying Raven along the archway that led to the empty building. Dragging his feet, Kez began to follow them.

The inside of the skyscraper section was equally unprepossessing. It was at least clean, though, and their footsteps echoed softly as they crossed the floor of the foyer. Four doors led off the main entrance hall and Finn showed Raven around conscientiously. The first door led into a large empty room that could be used for vehicles, the other three opened into stairways leading up to more empty rooms. After an initial exploration, Kez and Luciel returned to the entrance and sat down on the cold floor.

'It's not much like the apartment, is it?' Luciel said ruefully.

'I can't believe Raven agreed to move,' Kez replied bitterly. 'This area looks like a bomb site. We'll have to barricade ourselves in just to avoid the gangs, let alone the Seccies.'

The noise of flitters setting down outside alerted them to a new arrival and they looked up to see the two craft they'd seen at the Countess's base being loaded with Raven's equipment. As they watched, some of the Countess's people started taking crates out of the vehicles and began to carry them along the walkway.

'It looks like it's going to take Raven some time to get this place operational,' Luciel said.

'The longer the better,' Kez replied.

By the time Caitlin returned from the Gateshall school, Daniel had finished packing the small amount of stuff he intended to take with him and had written a note to his father. There wasn't much he could say, other than that he no longer felt comfortable with the privileged lifestyle he led in Belgravia and that he hoped his father would understand. Daniel didn't cherish much hope of that, but once he was hidden with Anglecynn his father would only see him again if they were discovered by the Security Services and he had to find some way to say goodbye. When Caitlin arrived back he was waiting for a commercial flitter to collect him, and his sister entered the apartment to find him in the main living room with his bags packed. Caitlin looked at him in surprise when she saw the bags.

'Hey, Daniel, what's going on?' she asked. 'Are you moving out or something?'

'I'm going to stay with some friends for a while,' Daniel told her. 'I've got a letter for you to give Father.'

'He doesn't know?' Caitlin was incredulous. 'Daniel, he's going to be furious when he finds out. Who are these friends anyway?'

'No one you know.' Daniel sighed, finding it harder than he'd expected to explain himself. 'Look, Caitlin, I know you don't think much about politics but try to understand, I'm just not comfortable living here now that Father runs the Security Services. I think that what they're doing is wrong, especially now that they're helping the CPS exterminate Hexes.'

'What do you mean?' Caitlin looked frightened. 'Working for the government is just a job – why should it matter to you what Father does? Why should you care about Hexes or the CPS?'

'Why should I care?' Daniel felt himself getting angry and attempted to control his temper. 'Caitlin, just because we've been lucky doesn't mean the rest of the world has nothing to do with us. All you've ever had to worry about is being pretty and popular. You've got no idea how many people have to fight to survive every day of their lives!'

'You're crazy.' Caitlin looked at him coldly. 'Why can't you just be normal, Daniel? There isn't anything you can do about poverty or injustice or anything like that so why do you have to act as if you're better than the rest of us?' Turning her back on him she headed for her room, saying over her shoulder: 'Go and be a martyr if you want to be. When you get bored you'll come back.'

Avalon couldn't remember a time when she didn't know she was a Hex. Brought up in the glitter and gold of clubland, the part of the city that was a playground for the rich and a prison for the poor, everything about Avalon's life had hovered on the edge of illegality. She'd never known her father, her mother danced in the stage shows the clubs put on and Avalon spent her childhood between the shining lights where the rich played and the slum apartment on the edge of gangland where the poor starved. Her mother's only gifts were her dancing and her prettiness and to escape the trap of the slums she hired herself to the clubs. But the drug and alcohol abuse that pervaded the slums and ganglands like a choking fog was also there in clubland, the same scent only sweetened with the tang of money.

She never knew for certain if her mother was aware that she possessed the mutant Hex gene, but throughout her childhood her mother taught her to hide what she was from other people.

'Whether you run with a gang or work for the rich, you can't ever let them know who you are,' her mother told her. 'Because then they have a part of you. You have wonderful gifts, Avalon, and you can be anything you want, just as long as you never let anyone else decide your future.'

And Avalon had done just that. With no official

identity or existence she couldn't have found a place in a school and so she learnt from the people who worked in clubland. All they had to teach was dance and music and how to sell your talents to the people who paid, but in the end that was enough. When Avalon's mother had died, spending their last savings on slum-doctors who didn't even attempt to cure her, Avalon had taken her place on stage. But where her mother's gifts had been only just enough to earn her that place, Avalon shone like a star. At fifteen her success had already been assured. From clubs to concert-halls and stadia, she had rocketed to mega-stardom, keeping her secrets for herself. Now she was on the pinnacle of that success, admired by millions, envied by billions, but despite fame and fortune still afraid that some day she would be found out.

Touching the moment control, she played the news item again. In silence, for by now she knew the words off by heart and she whispered them to herself as the pictures flickered in front of her.

'. . . pledged the Security Services to a widespread eradication programme, supporting the CPS in their mandate to rid this country of Hexes for ever.'

She touched the control again and the picture froze in position as Avalon picked up her guitar. Her fingers moved softly across the strings, and chords rang out from the amp across the room, melding seamlessly with the images in Avalon's mind. As the music began to form a pattern, she wondered, as she often did, if she needed to touch the strings. But, as always, you never knew who might be watching, or when it was dangerous to forget the rules. So she played conventionally, the only clue to her abilities being the perfection of her music – the way each note seemed exactly right for that moment. The song she was composing was dangerous enough, but she had told Cloud she was thinking of composing something with a terrorist theme and it was time for her to deliver. Lyrics could come later, for now it was a sound she was looking for. Something that would wordlessly express the emotions she would only ever use words to conceal.

Wraith had spent the day with Revenge, as he was increasingly forced to think of her. Even while he called her Rachel, to her face and in front of the others, he had begun to realize that she would never be Rachel again. The image he had held in his mind through all those years of searching, the kid with shining brown eyes and a crooked grin, had been erased by Dr Kalden's experimentation, leaving behind the gaunt and silent figure he tended now. Revenge was the memory of Rachel and a constant source of guilt. He couldn't even look at her without thinking of how he had failed. He had failed Rachel by not finding her soon enough, failed Raven in allowing her to distance herself from the world and failed the other Hexes he hadn't been able to rescue in the raid on the lab.

Sadly, he watched Revenge, still enmeshed in a tangle of machinery, although this time it was of her own choice. When they'd first moved into the apartment, Raven had fitted her sister's room with the medical equipment necessary to help her through the withdrawal symptoms of the drugs she was kept on, a bank of vidscreens for entertainment and a VR Helmet system to play computer games without having to move her wasted limbs. Wraith had argued that they should try to get her to come out and rejoin the world but Raven had overruled him.

'That might be what you want for her, but it's not what she wants,' she told him. 'She wants to hide, inside this room and inside her own mind. She's Revenge now, not Rachel – don't remind her of what she can't have.'

So now, except for the physiotherapy sessions she had once a day, Revenge remained cocooned in her mechanical world.

Wraith stroked her hand, not expecting a response, and stood up. Ali was still in the main room of the apartment and he knew he ought to spend time with her. He could hardly ignore the fact that Ali was miserable here and he couldn't risk failing her as he felt he had failed so many others.

As he left Revenge's room he heard the sound of an arrival and glancing at the main door he saw Raven, Luciel and Kez enter. The boys looked subdued but Raven was grinning.

'I've found us a place,' she informed him, slinging her black rucksack onto a nearby chair and kicking her heavy boots off. 'It'll take me a couple of weeks to get it fixed up properly, but after that we'll have a better security system than the Countess. She's already hired me to refit hers when I'm through.'

'Congratulations,' Wraith said, with relief. He'd always been uneasy living so openly in the heights of the city, especially now that they all had so much to hide. He and Kez were the only members of the groups whose existence wasn't illegal and both of them were still wanted for the attack on the lab. Now it looked as if he was going to have his wish and he was grateful to Raven for no longer opposing him. 'So, what next then?'

'What about this training programme for Hexes?' Kez asked diffidently. 'It would be useful if Luciel and Ali could do some of the stuff you do.' He looked hopefully at Raven.

'If they can,' Raven said drily, but before the others

could protest she held up a hand. 'But I agree. We'll start just as soon as I've contacted Avalon. I still need more data on the Hex abilities and my observations indicate that she is a fully functioning Hex.'

'How are you going to contact her?' Ali asked, showing an interest in the conversation for the first time.

'Wouldn't you like to know?' Raven grinned mischievously.

'Raven . . .' Wraith began, warningly, but she interrupted him.

'Stay ice, Wraith, it's under control.' She smiled. 'If all goes well I should meet her tonight.' She looked round at the rest of them. 'As things are I think I'll have to go on my own, though – too many of you are wanted criminals.'

'And you're not?' Ali exclaimed. She looked at Wraith, hopefully. 'I think I should go,' she said. 'I know media people and how to talk to them.'

Raven looked contemptuous but Wraith was thoughtful.

'Wouldn't you be recognized?' he asked carefully. 'Your father was quite prominent and your arrest was widely reported.'

'I could change the way I look,' Ali persisted. 'Maybe if I coloured my hair . . .'

'I don't think Raven should go on her own,' Kez put in. 'I could go with her.'

'I don't need protection,' Raven insisted. 'All I'm doing is going to a party I think Avalon will be at. It's not exactly dangerous.'

'Take the younger ones, then,' Wraith replied. 'I agree I'm likely to be recognized but Luciel isn't and Kez or Ali could be disguised.'

Raven considered this for a moment, then shrugged.

'Come if you want,' she said eventually. 'But I'm not

going to be watching over you all the time – and make sure you don't get in my way. You're old enough to take care of yourselves.'

Luciel and Kez agreed quickly, excited to be involved for a change, and after a moment Ali did too. She resented Raven treating her like a kid when she was older than her, but she wanted to be included as much as the others.

'OK, then,' Raven agreed. 'Don't dress too noticeably and be ready to leave in two hours. If you're not ready, I'll leave without you.' And, with that, she stalked off to her room, closing the door decisively behind her.

Alaric was asleep in the small room he shared with Jordan when he was woken by the chime of the vidcom. Dragging himself wearily out of bed, he crossed the room to answer it and saw Liz staring back at him.

'Maggie and Cal have brought in your new recruit,' she informed him. 'Daniel Hammond.'

'Oh yeah,' Alaric nodded, starting to rub the sleep out of his eyes.

'He's in the debriefing room,' Liz added and broke the connection, the vidcom screen going dark.

Alaric got up and stretched. He'd been asleep in his clothes; the building's heat units had been malfunctioning again and everyone was too busy to fix them. Pulling on his battered jacket, he headed downstairs. He'd promised Daniel Hammond a place here; the least he could do was greet him.

The debriefing room was a small office with a table and chairs and little else. Daniel Hammond was standing uneasily near the table, rubbing his hands to keep them warm, a couple of expensive suitcases next to him. A cup of coffee substitute was cooling on the table nearby. For an instant Alaric looked at their base as Daniel must see it. A dreary island in a sea of garbage, cold and inhospitable and reeking of poverty. But he refused to accept the image. His job was to make the new recruit feel welcome and to do that he had to concentrate on the positive aspects of the home they had here.

'Daniel Hammond?' he said with a welcoming smile. 'I'm Alaric. I wasn't able to tell you my name when we first met. But now you've officially joined us, you ought to know who we are.'

'Pleased to meet you,' Daniel replied, obviously trying to look relaxed.

'And there are a lot of people who'll be pleased to meet you,' Alaric replied. 'Your information has been very useful to us. Why don't you sit down and I'll explain some things, then I'll show you around.' As Daniel slid into one of the rickety chairs, Alaric drew another up to the table and began the introduction he'd given to every new recruit.

'As you're probably already aware, Anglecynn isn't a large organization – at the moment we number about fifty – but every member is dedicated and prepared to commit themselves to our goals. This is our main base, but we have other contacts in the city and a few sympathizers in the rest of Britain. We don't have a hierarchy as such, but the longer you've been with the organization the more qualified you are considered to be and the greater role you have in deciding our strategies. Not everyone here takes part in the protests and demonstrations we organize; we have about ten administrative staff who are responsible for our research and the preparation for events. It'll be up to you to fit in where you feel the most comfortable. We call this place Dragon's Nest and there's plenty of space for everyone so you can either move in to a shared room or find one for yourself. Nowhere's out of bounds and if you get in anyone's way they'll tell you about it. The common room's where most of us spend our free time and hold meetings when there's something to discuss.' He leaned back and considered his words for a moment, thinking over what he had said. Daniel was nodding, but he still looked nervous and Alaric decided putting him at his ease was the priority.

'That's about all you need to know now but if you have any other questions ask anyone or come and find me. If you can't find me, ask for Jordan – she's my girlfriend and she usually knows how to get hold of me. She's also one of our veterans and can sort you out on most things herself.' Standing up he put a reassuring hand on Daniel's shoulder. 'Now, if you want to have a look around, I'll give you the grand tour.'

'Thank you,' Daniel said, his smile looking a bit more genuine. He reached a hand into his pocket and pulled out a few disks. 'What about these? It's the data you wanted – shall I give them to you now?'

'Sure,' Alaric replied, taking them easily. But as they left the debriefing room he knew that, once he'd showed Daniel around, he'd have to start work right away on them. It would be a long time before he got another chance to sleep.

4
Subtler than Vulcan's Engine

The party Raven had decided to crash was the ultimate in celebrity glitzfests. Held in the infamous Winter Palace, an exclusive club at the peak of one of the tallest of the high-rises, the ostensible purpose of the event was to celebrate Elohim's thirtieth birthday but in actuality the get-together was to convince everyone that the star was still the paramount talent of the day, despite recent ratings losses to Yannis Kastell and Masque. The Winter Palace had been chosen as the venue, not least because it resembled something from Elohim's own holovids. Its crystalline walls, designed to simulate the effects of snow and frost, sparkled in the starlight and a flurry of holographic snowflakes whirled around the arriving flitters, projected by holocams mounted on the towering parapets, spires and flying buttresses of the palace.

Raven had rented a state-of-the-art customized flitter for the purpose and, as she piloted the small craft in to land on one of the castle's projecting crystalline platforms, her three passengers stared out of the darkened windows in awe. Ali knew all about the Winter Palace but even she had never thought she'd visit it. Kez and Luciel gaped in wide-eyed wonder at the fairy-tale structure. When the flitter landed and Raven stepped out, the others followed uneasily, feeling under-dressed and out of place. Raven alone looked at her ease. Wearing dead black as usual, she didn't at first seem to have made any special effort, but in the glittering lights of the Winter Palace the others could see that her clothes were made of a light-retarding fabric that retained its obsidian darkness even under the multiple floodlight reflections, seeming to clothe her in shadows. The others were also dressed plainly and Ali's ash-blond hair had been dyed a dark chestnut in keeping with their attempt at disguise. Following Raven to the end of the spur that joined the flitter platform to the palace itself, they exchanged worried looks as a burly security guard stepped forward to confront Raven.

'ID please, m'am,' he said, reaching for a small vid-unit hanging at his belt, which undoubtedly held a copy of the invitation list.

'Elizabeth Black,' Raven told him calmly, then turned to indicate the rest of them. 'Lestan Austen, Annabel Tarrant and Kester Chirac.'

'Thank you, m'am,' the guard replied, scanning through the names on his list. After a brief moment he looked up with a polite smile and stepped aside to let them pass. 'Have a nice evening.'

The interior decoration of the Winter Palace was equally fantastical, every surface glittering with frosty silver light. For this occasion vidscreens had been mounted all over the walls and cycled through scenes from Elohim's latest vids. Holo units were mounted on balconies and staircases, projecting images of imaginary alien creatures which mixed with the throng of celebrities who filled the halls. Watching this from the high balcony which led to the flitter platform, Raven smiled to herself, then turned to regard the others.

'You can go and mingle,' she told them. 'Don't draw too much attention to yourselves.'

'What are you going to do?' Ali asked curiously.

'Get an introduction to Avalon.'

Avalon had made her entrance, with the other members of Masque, in full view of the media. Little flitters circled the Winter Palace, recording the arrival of the various celebrities for the news networks, and a few dedicated fans filled other larger craft which swarmed around the entrance. The phalanx of bodyguards, hired to protect the members of the rock group from unwanted attention, formed a protective knot around them as their flitter touched down on the most secure of the palace's landing platforms.

Once inside, Corin and Jesse peeled off in search of refreshment while the other three surveyed the crowd. Avalon felt almost overpowered by the scene. Elohim had intended this celebration to impress and as his music filled the air and his face flickered from the multiple screens, Avalon found it difficult to remember that she was now as big a star as he was. Cloud evidently had no such problem. Poised elegantly at the side of the main hall, he accepted a glass of pale gold wine from a passing waiter and sipped it casually.

'Quite a show,' he said softly. 'I'm surprised Elohim wants to remind so many people of how old he is.'

'He's not that old,' Lissa protested. 'It's not as if he's exactly losing his looks, even if his talent is a little in doubt these days.'

'You know that, but does he?' Cloud replied speculatively. 'At thirty I'd start to get just a little nervous about birthdays.'

'Are you going to tell him that?' Lissa asked, her eyes sparkling at the thought of a confrontation.

'Certainly not,' Cloud replied, beckoning to another waiter and gesturing to him to serve Avalon and Lissa. 'I shall be perfectly gracious. There's no need to say anything. Everyone here knows that we're at the top of the ratings again.' Ignoring Lissa's attempt to continue the conversation, he took Avalon's arm and began to lead her across the room. 'Don't look so nervous,' he said quietly. 'Remember you're a megastar.'

'I don't like this kind of thing,' she replied, under her breath. 'I feel like the main dish at a banquet.'

'Elohim's the dish of the day,' Cloud said, smiling. 'He's over there with his dedicated admirers, all paying court to the Prince of the Vidscreen.'

Avalon turned to look at Elohim, dressed in silver and white, smiling generously at the host of admirers who clustered around him. Her gaze lingered on the group for a moment then, almost against her will, was arrested by a dark figure making her way across the hall towards Elohim. Alone in this glittering company she wore black and, against her pale skin and onyx hair, it made her look as if there was no colour to her at all. Other heads were turning and Avalon recognized how that much blackness would inevitably catch the eye in a room full of light.

'Who's that?' she whispered to Cloud.

'No idea,' he replied. 'Looks like she's lost the way to a funeral.'

'Elohim seems to know her,' she continued as the dark-haired girl was greeted by the megastar. Cloud shrugged and, with one last glance at the stranger, Avalon turned away.

Across the room Ali had also noticed Raven's progress towards the megastar, at first with alarm and then with a surge of jealousy as Elohim greeted her with a warm smile of recognition. Thinking back to a life that seemed decades ago now, she remembered how Elohim had put in an appearance at one of her father's parties. Raven had been there as well, masquerading under a pseudonym, the first time Ali had met the young Hex. Ali had never imagined that Elohim would actually remember her but now he was talking to Raven and smiling as if he'd known her all her life, while Ali was left in a corner unrecognized and unnoticed. It didn't do her any good to remember that she'd deliberately come in disguise; she doubted that anyone here would have given her a second glance if she'd introduced herself as Ali Tarrell. But Raven had the gift of being noticed and a supreme confidence in her own abilities. Ali's eyes defocused as she watched the crowd blindly, wondering if she would be in Raven's shadow for the rest of her life.

Meanwhile, Elohim was leading Raven across the room, towards Avalon and Cloud. There was a touch of pique in his voice as he asked:

'Why do you want to meet her anyway? Masque have made a few discs but they're hardly known outside this country.'

'I'm researching a programme on minor European groups,' Raven replied with a sideways smile. 'I heard about Masque recently and thought they might be useful material.'

'I see.' Elohim lost his frown as he guided Raven towards Avalon, acknowledging other people's greetings with an expansive smile.

Pacing beside him, Raven's dark eyes were alight with amusement. It had all been so easy. Hacking into the system which held the invitation list was the work of moments and reviving her Elizabeth Black identity had secured her an introduction to Avalon and the status of knowing Elohim. The fact that the megastar was obviously interested in her only served to increase her amusement and she had to prevent herself from grinning as they came close to Avalon.

Avalon wore dark red, the same colour as her flame of crimson hair. As she looked up to see Elohim approaching, Raven felt a shock of recognition. She felt that she would have known Avalon as a Hex even if she hadn't already surmised it from Masque's music. Watching as Elohim greeted her, Raven attempted to clarify her own impressions, trying to understand her own certainty about Avalon. But, apart from that sensation of recognition, she had nothing to go on and she filed the incident away for further study. Elohim was introducing her and she had to concentrate on the business at hand.

'This is Elizabeth Black, a friend of mine,' Elohim said proprietorially.

'I'm assistant producer for AdAstra,' Raven continued. 'It's a pleasure to meet you. I've been following your career with great interest.'

'Really?' Avalon studied Raven with candid consideration. 'What do you think of it?'

Elohim drifted away towards a group of holo executives, uninterested in a conversation about Masque's music, as Raven began to answer.

'I assume you want more than a personal criticism,' she said and smiled as Avalon nodded. 'In that case, my main impression is that your apocalyptic imagery suggests that Masque is on the brink of a transformation, although apocalypse usually signals an ending rather than a beginning.'

'You think Masque's career is ending?' Avalon said quickly, her violet eyes darkening.

'No,' Raven corrected her. 'I think you do.'

'Masque has no intention of splitting up,' Avalon replied, stating categorically in case her comments got back to the media.

'The future is always uncertain,' Raven replied before adding quietly, 'And none of us is ever really safe. Even me, though my associates would be surprised to hear me admit it.'

'What do you mean?' Avalon said quickly, glancing around to see if anyone else was nearby.

'We're alone,' Raven replied. 'In more ways than one.' Her dark eyes met Avalon's levelly. 'But, if you let me teach you, you won't be defenceless.' Reaching into her jacket she produced a small metal card. 'My com signal's encoded into this,' she explained, passing it to Avalon. 'Ask for Raven.'

Before Avalon could reply she had stepped away, a shadow drifting through the brightness of the crowd.

Kez and Luciel were watching the party from an upper balcony. They had seen Raven approach Elohim, and Kez explained that Raven had met the megastar before, even though he was amazed at her audacity. They continued to watch as Elohim took Raven to meet Avalon and had seen the young hacker give something to the singer before turning and coming back across the hall towards them. They came down the staircase to meet her and she greeted them with a grin.

'I've seen her,' she said. 'Shall we go now or are you enjoying the experience?'

'I don't think we should push our luck,' Luciel said, reluctantly. Kez was more decisive.

'Let's leave,' he said. 'These people don't seem real at all. It's like watching them on a vid.'

'I'm not sure many of them can tell the difference either,' Raven agreed. 'Where's Ali?'

'Over there,' Luciel pointed out. 'She doesn't look like she's enjoying herself much.'

'Probably missing the high life,' Kez said.

'Go and get her then, Luciel,' Raven instructed. 'We'll fade and meet you at the flitter.'

Alaric pushed his chair back from the computer terminal and stretched painfully. Glancing at the chronometer he realized he'd been working for hours, checking and rechecking the information Daniel had brought them. The reference in the Security Minister's notes to extra surveillance in the ganglands and increased Seccie 'stop and searches' had worried him, but it was the information on the Hex terrorist faction that had been the focus of his work. The description of the terrorists and the name Raven had appeared on the newscasts, but the reference to missing test subjects was a new factor.

He'd searched the net for more information on the 'CPS Facility' the terrorists had allegedly destroyed and found no information even on its existence until it had been blown up, when its location was given and it was described as an extermination centre. The mention of test subjects caused Alaric to doubt that and also explained why the group had chosen to target that particular facility rather than any of the hundreds of others scattered across the country. Even more interesting was the note Daniel had appended to the files mentioning that Ali Tarrell, described as a missing test subject, was a teenage Hex who was listed as legally exterminated by the CPS. It looked to Alaric as if the 'terrorist raid' had in fact been a rescue attempt and it made him increasingly eager to make contact with the group. Unfortunately, if the group had half the resources they would have needed to mount an assault on a test lab no one even knew existed, they would be difficult to track down.

Alaric considered the problem as he made arrangements for countering the increased Seccie activity, instituting new recognition codes and protocols and restricting all members of the group to Dragon's Nest except for essential business. Eventually he decided he couldn't think of anything but turning the problem over to the fixers. Throughout the slums and ganglands there were fixers who claimed to be able to set up any contact or provide any equipment. Chances were the Hex group had encountered one of them and could pass on a message. Starting with fixers in London, Alaric sent a coded message to each of them, indicating Anglecynn's interest in meeting up with the Hexes.

Finally leaving the terminal, he went to find Jordan. She and Daniel were in the main common room and Alaric was relieved to find that the new recruit was looking a bit less nervous. Although Daniel was slightly older than him, Alaric had spent half his life on the edge of the law and he knew how protected from reality those who grew up in the heights were. Jordan was one of the best people to help him come to terms with life in the depths of the city. She'd come from the heights herself; studying politics at school had involved her in a number of political protests and got her into trouble with the Seccies. By the time she'd met up with Anglecynn she'd already had a hard lesson in what the city was actually like. As he sank into the chair beside her, Alaric felt himself begin to relax. Even in the depths of the darkness he still had hope.

*

Revenge, immersed in her own personal and private darkness, had no hope at all. She existed in shadows now and everything she experienced seemed to take place a long way away, receding from view like light seen from the end of a dark tunnel. Even Wraith was like a phantom to her, more memory than reality. But Raven was real and sometimes Revenge could convince herself that she *was* Raven, able to drive the darkness away. Somewhere out in the dark Dr Kalden was looking for her and he wouldn't stop looking ever. The only thing that prevented her from whimpering in fright was the thought of revenge, that next time she would be stronger. Now as she lay on her back she repeated her incantation.

'I am Raven,' she whispered into the dark, 'and Raven is Revenge.' The darkness seemed to lift a little and Revenge's breathing calmed. If Kalden was looking for her, she would hunt him, and this time there would be no escape.

Wraith, looking in on the sleeping figure of his little sister, was startled to see the smile on her lips. Allowing himself to hope it was a sign she was recovering, he gently pulled the covers over the sleeping figure. Turning on a small light by her bed, he keyed down the main lights, remembering how hysterical she'd been the one time he'd turned them all off at once. In the dark he could see that the lights of the room's computer terminal were on and reminded himself to speak to Raven about it. If Revenge felt able to use the net it might be a sign that the scars, from her experience in the lab, were fading. As he left the room, he felt the burden of guilt he carried lift a little.

When Raven returned to the apartment with the others she didn't show much inclination to talk. Wraith hadn't waited up for them and Ali had quickly headed for her room. While Kez and Luciel turned on the holovid, Raven had left them for the privacy of her room. For the next few hours she worked in silence with the tangle of circuitry she was gradually assembling into a computer link of her own design. Only her occasional glance at the terminal betrayed that her attention was divided. It was late into the night when the com signal finally chimed and Raven crossed the room to touch the keypad. She had given Avalon a coded signal, the circuitry in the card sending her message through multiple relay stations before bringing it to Raven's attention, all in the space of microseconds. She hadn't thought the singer would want to betray herself by reporting her, but Raven didn't trust anyone entirely.

Her fingers dancing across the keypad, she instructed the unit to key the incoming signal while suppressing the outgoing visual signal. Avalon's face appeared on screen. Her red hair was dishevelled but her expression was calm.

'Is that Raven?' she asked quietly, dim light in the background indicating that she was making the call in secret.

Through her link with the system, Raven checked that the signal was not being monitored and keyed the terminal to display her image.

'This is Raven,' she confirmed. 'I've been expecting your call.'

'Are you really the hacker?' Avalon frowned. 'Elohim said your name was Elizabeth.'

'I am Raven,' she replied and wordlessly extended her consciousness through the link. She felt the sensation of speed as part of her identity raced through the same convoluted route as Avalon's signal, tracing the link back to its point of origin. Although Avalon had not consciously entered the data network, part of her mind responded automatically to the presence of the circuitry, her Hex gene giving her a part of the symbiotic union Raven had with the network. It was enough for Raven to touch her mind through the terminal, confirming her assertion with the wordless message:

> I am Raven <

Avalon tensed, her eyes glazing over for a fraction of a second before returning to reality.

'What do you want from me?' she asked and through the network Raven sensed **> fear <**.

'To learn from you,' Raven informed her, not attempting to conceal her intentions. Unlike Wraith, she doubted the possibility of forming a solidarity group of mutants but the existence of another functioning Hex fascinated her.

'I want to understand more about the potential of our kind,' she told Avalon. 'In return I offer to teach you what I know.'

'What do you think you can learn from me?' Avalon asked.

'You use your talents more artistically than me.' Raven gave a half-smile. 'My interests have been in other directions. Why shouldn't we learn from each other?' Reaching through her link with the net, she added:

> i can teach/show/give you this <

'What would I have to do?' Avalon asked, her expression unreadable.

'Meet with my associates?' Raven suggested. 'There are things you might want to know about the CPS.'

'It sounds dangerous,' Avalon said seriously.

'You can decide on a meeting place,' Raven told her.

Avalon was silent for a minute, obviously thinking, before she spoke again.

'The Carlisle Hotel, tomorrow at midday,' she said eventually.

'I'll arrange a room,' Raven confirmed. 'You can find me under the name Aria Draven.'

As Avalon cut the connection, Raven withdrew from the net, then hesitated. Within the terminals connected to the apartment she felt a difference. Tracing it back to its source, her awareness concentrated on the terminal in Revenge's room. Unused since their occupancy began it was now showing signs of use. Drawing closer Raven found the traces of activity; some of the operating code had been changed. The alterations were confusing; a babel of new code threaded through the system, disappearing and reappearing as Raven tried to track it down. Raven raised an eyebrow. Apparently the Hex abilities the CPS had found in Rachel were resurfacing in Revenge after lying hidden since her rescue from the lab. Raven recorded the snatches of code on her own terminal, simultaneously imprinting them on her eidetic memory and slid out of the net. She would have to talk to Revenge soon, she told herself, before crossing the room to fall asleep in seconds.

By the time Ali got up the next day, the others were already planning their meeting with Avalon. Wraith was insistent that recruiting her would be the first step towards a campaign on behalf of the Hexes. Raven was more sceptical but the fact that she'd convinced the megastar to meet with them had let loose a new enthusiasm in the other members of the group. Luciel took advantage of the opportunity to ask Raven when she would start teaching them to use their Hex abilities.

'After I've spoken to Avalon,' she replied. 'The things I

intend to tell her will be the basis of your education as well.'

'It sounds as if you've progressed in understanding Hex abilities,' Wraith said carefully.

Raven grimaced, then shook her head.

'Not enough,' she said. 'The disks I took from the lab were worse than useless. They spent too much time exploring blind alleys of experimentation and all their subjects were too immature.'

'They were kids,' Luciel said sharply.

'I'm not being callous,' Raven said coldly. 'I am criticizing the scientific methodology, which is separate from ethical considerations. In any case,' she continued, 'I got a little information from the tests – although mostly what avenues not to follow – some ideas from talking to Ali and Luciel and a little more from Revenge. Discovering Avalon has been useful as well. What I'll say to her today includes my current hypothesis concerning the Hex gene.' Swinging her boots down from the table she headed towards her room, turning over her shoulder to add: 'By the way, someone should stay with Revenge today. It could be unwise to leave her on her own.'

The door of Raven's room closed, making it clear she didn't consider herself a candidate for remaining behind. The three younger members of the group glanced at Wraith and then at each other. Kez was the first to reach the obvious conclusion.

'Wraith and Raven have to go and you two are Hexes,' he said. 'I guess I'll stay behind.' Luciel flashed him a smile but Ali's expression was glum. To his surprise Kez found himself wishing that he carried the mutant gene, now that it looked as if Raven was going to start teaching the others. Looking at Ali's expression he couldn't understand why she wasn't more enthusiastic about the idea. As it was, looking after Revenge at least didn't present much of a chore, he told himself. It wasn't as if she was likely to go anywhere.

The suite Raven had booked at the Carlisle Hotel was luxurious and secluded and the hotel had a reputation for discretion. While Raven used the terminal to access the hotel's security system, in order to watch for the approach of Seccies or the CPS, the others tried to make themselves comfortable. They had arrived some time before they were due to meet with Avalon, and Wraith began scanning the newsfeeds for any more information on the security services' crackdown.

Ali and Luciel had nothing to do but wait. Neither of them was sure what Raven intended to say to the megastar or to them.

'It's hard to believe Avalon is a Hex,' Luciel said quietly. 'The CPS seem to catch most of us as kids.'

'They didn't catch Raven,' Ali said, with a touch of bitterness. 'That's probably why she's so interested in Avalon. We were both caught but she managed to stay unnoticed.'

'You think that's why?' Luciel asked, lowering his voice even further.

'Do you remember what I told you when we first met in the lab?' Ali asked.

'Something about Raven?' Luciel frowned, then shook his head. 'Sorry, I don't remember.'

'I told you what she told me,' Ali replied softly. 'Anyone able to escape the CPS wouldn't want to burden themselves with people who aren't.' She glanced over at Raven, but the younger girl appeared to be completely absorbed in the terminal. 'She didn't even want to take the other test subjects with us when we left the lab.'

'She couldn't have done,' Luciel protested. 'I know what I said at the time, but I didn't know how small your group was then. I still feel guilty that we didn't try. But we couldn't have saved them. And Raven *did* contact the media.'

'I know.' Ali's expression was bleak. 'But she didn't care, did she? Not like us, and not the way Wraith does.'

'She's just different,' Luciel said, but his voice was edged with uncertainty.

'Look at all the effort she's going to just to meet Avalon,' Ali pointed out. 'She doesn't care about us because we got caught or about Rev— Rachel, because her brain is fried. But she thinks Avalon is worth the effort.'

'Raven cares about some people, like Wraith, or Kez – she rescued him from the streets.'

'No, she didn't,' Ali insisted, her voice rising. 'Wraith did. Kez just thinks Raven did it because he has a crush on her.'

'What about Wraith then?' Luciel continued. 'Do you really think Raven doesn't feel anything for him? He's her brother.'

'Rachel is her sister, but she doesn't seem to feel anything for her,' Ali replied. 'She thinks of her as a test subject, just like—' She stopped abruptly when Luciel interrupted.

'Like Dr Kalden? No chance,' he insisted in a furious whisper. 'I know you don't get on with Raven and I admit she doesn't seem to think much of us as Hexes. But you weren't in the lab for long, Ali – you don't know what Kalden was like. Raven might be cold, but she's not *evil*!'

Ali looked away for a moment and then sighed.

'I'm sorry,' she said quietly. 'I don't mean to be unfair. I'm just tired of being so useless.'

Silently Luciel took her hand and held it. There wasn't anything he could say and they both knew it.

Avalon arrived three minutes after midday. Raven saw her arriving through the hotel's security cams. She was alone, pulling up in a plain black skimmer, her distinctive red hair tucked under a cap. Raven watched her passage through the hotel, different holocams picking her up in the foyer, elevator and corridor on their floor. She was impressed by what she saw. Avalon betrayed no sign of nervousness. Only Raven, familiar with the constant anxiety of having to hide her mutation, would have been able to see any tension in the star's deliberate movements. Smiling to herself she turned away from the terminal.

'She's on her way up,' she said. 'No one accompanying her, no signs of pursuit or surveillance.'

'Good.' Wraith relaxed perceptibly and turned off the holovid, crossing to sit with the others in the suite's lounge area. Ali and Luciel were looking apprehensive and neither of them met his eyes as he joined them. Raven continued to watch the terminal for a few moments more. Then she got up, the terminal switching itself off without her apparently touching it, and crossed to the door. She was halfway there when they heard a soft knock, sounding as loud as a hammer in the suddenly silent room.

Raven opened the door and the others looked up expectantly as she ushered Avalon in, closing the door behind her. The star's eyes skimmed across the group quickly before coming back to Raven.

'These are your associates?' she asked. 'I was expecting something more militaristic.'

'We're not terrorists,' Raven replied. 'Despite our reputations.' Gesturing to Avalon to sit down, she came to sit next to Wraith. 'This is my brother, Wraith; and Ali Tarrell and Luciel Liechtmann; both Hexes.'

'Avalon,' the redhead said politely, nodding to each of them.

'We're pleased you could find the time to meet with us,' Wraith began, taking charge of the situation. 'As Raven pointed out, our reputations are against us. I know that she has promised you certain information. But I'd like to begin by explaining how we came to possess it.'

He looked expectantly at Avalon, who nodded.

'I'd rather have the full story,' she said calmly.

'In that case I'll begin by saying that Raven and I have a younger sister and we first came to this city to discover what had become of her . . .'

Avalon listened in silence as Wraith recounted the results of their search for Rachel, Raven's discovery of the illegal experimentation and their meeting with Ali. Reluctant to remember the past, Ali briefly explained how she had acted as a spy in the laboratory and left it to Luciel to describe the facility and the details of the experiments. Wraith took up the story once more to describe their attempt to expose the CPS by calling in the media and the subsequent explosion that had destroyed the lab, resulting in the government branding them as terrorists.

'Everyone died,' Luciel couldn't help himself from adding. 'Dr Kalden destroyed the evidence so that no one would find him out.'

'We don't know it was Kalden for certain,' Wraith interjected.

'It's not as if it makes much difference,' Ali said. 'Everyone blamed it on us.'

'And now the government has vowed to eliminate all Hexes as a result,' Avalon concluded.

5
Cover her Face

Kez was trying not to feel bored but it was difficult when the others had gone to meet Avalon and all he had to do was look after Revenge. He'd checked on her four times, apart from taking her breakfast or lunch, but each time she'd either been wired up to her VR Helmet or her computer terminal. Despite Kez's attempts, she hadn't spoken to him once and he wondered, as always, if she would ever have a chance of leading a normal life. Shaking his head he returned to the living room, dialling himself a snack from the Nutromac.

'Raven, Wraith and Revenge,' he said under his breath. 'What a family.' To his surprise the thought cheered him up. Revenge might be weird, but he was starting to believe that Raven and Wraith could do anything. Kez had never joined a gang when he was living on the streets, distrusting the loyalty gang members claimed to have towards each other. But since he'd met Wraith and Raven he'd felt for the first time as if he belonged to something. His friendship with Luciel and even his quarrels with Ali were beginning to feel routine and familiar, like something he'd miss if he left the group.

'Like this apartment,' he reminded himself. While he'd been uncomfortable at Elohim's celebrity glitzfest, places like the Belgravia complex and this apartment were luxuries he'd be unwilling to give up. The talk of a move to ganglands had alarmed him, but remembering Raven's own taste for comfort he hoped they'd be able to refit the building to something like the luxury they had here. All the same, he'd still miss it. With a sigh, Kez stretched out along one of the long sofas and reached for the moment control, telling himself he might as well enjoy it while he could.

'Everyone's in danger,' Raven said. 'And we are one of the causes.' She looked round at the others. 'But I am the primary reason for the government's crackdown. Dr Kalden studied Hexes for most of his life. If his knowledge had been greater or his methodology more sound he might have discovered what he was searching for – a way to turn unwanted mutants into military superiority. He suspected that the Hexes possessed a capability to interface directly with electronics, something which would be of immense use in the art of war, but he never proved his theories. His subjects were too young, too few escaped detection as children and those that did were never found.'

Avalon's eyes were fixed on Raven; Ali and Luciel were similarly transfixed. Wraith watched the tableau silently, listening as the pent-up fury that was always present in Raven found release in her catalogue of discoveries.

'The only thing Kalden did discover was how to spur the Hex gene into action. Usually our capabilities are dormant. That accounts for the number of Hexes disposed of shortly after birth as a result of routine medical scans. But sometimes the gene passes undetected and Hexes are caught before adolescence, when anomalies are discovered during their interactions with electronic devices or as a result of further medical testing. These first two groups accounted for most of Kalden's subjects.

Through what amounted to torture he found ways of unlocking that potential, which is what happened to Rachel – she had no use of her abilities until after Kalden's experimentation. In a few cases his victims were teenagers who had begun to use their abilities themselves as a result of a particular interest in an electronic medium.

'But Kalden never had the opportunity to experiment on a subject who had reached adulthood and gained the full possession of their abilities. Avalon is the one person I know of who's even approached those criteria.'

'What about you?' Luciel interjected and Raven shrugged.

'I took my age into calculation when I started looking at Kalden's results. I discovered my abilities when I was nine and have been using them ever since. According to Dr Kalden's test results, my abilities significantly exceed those recorded for any age group. This is based on my study so far. Once I've attempted to teach you what I know, I'll be better able to reach a conclusion as to whether the extent of my abilities is unique or if the things I have learnt can be taught to any and all Hexes.'

Turning to Avalon she concluded:

'I am already committed to instructing Luciel and Ali, but your contribution would give me more information to go on, apart from proving useful if this new initiative leads to your discovery.'

Avalon was silent for a while, frowning to herself. Never before had she been inclined to go against her instincts and share her secrets with another person. But Raven seemed to know them already.

'I was a child when I found out I was a Hex. I can't ever remember not knowing. But I've never known how to use it, not as you do. I feel it sometimes in my music, in the way I use instruments, but I've never dared take it any further. I suppose my success has protected me from having to find out what I could do.' She looked at Ali and Luciel. 'Do you want to be able to use it? From what you've told me this could be more dangerous than any of us imagine.'

'I want to learn,' Luciel assured her. 'The government is wrong to think the mutation is harmful. Sure, it could be used for harm and the world relies on the security of the networks. But it's wrong to kill us for possessing a talent most people don't have. I want to learn to use it so I can prove that. Before this happened I was going to be a scientist. The only person I can experiment on is me.'

Ali listened to Luciel enviously. Discovering she was a Hex had seemed like the end of her life and she wished she could see the potential he did in the discovery.

'I just want to protect myself,' she admitted. 'The CPS caught me once – next time I want a chance to escape. If they're going to hunt me until I'm dead for being a Hex, I want to know what I can do to defend myself.'

'Wraith, you should answer too,' Raven said softly. 'It's possible that since Rachel and I had the potential, you do as well. There are tests I'd like to do.'

'Of course,' Wraith answered immediately. He looked at the others. 'If I am a Hex it won't make much difference to my life. Besides I'm already committed to fighting the government as long as the extermination laws exist.'

'You make it sound like the only possible decision.' Avalon smiled wistfully. 'I'm going to have to think about it. I've been hiding this all my life and if I start to use it, I don't know where I'll stop.'

'It has to be your decision,' Wraith agreed, but Raven's eyes were dark with premonition.

'You've begun already,' she said. 'When you're ready to admit it, contact us.'

Revenge wasn't even aware of Kez's presence although she noticed every once in a while that someone had brought food. She ate it without interest. It was the computer terminal that drew her attention. She had seen it when they first brought her to this room, squatting in the corner like a spider waiting for a fly. She wanted to use it, to touch it, but for a long time she had been able to escape its trap. The monitors by the bed were frightening but Raven had put them there and Raven was safe. Raven had also brought the helmet and that was safe too. With the helmet she didn't have to be Raven or Revenge, she could just be, in a world of colour where it was never dark. But the helmet wasn't real, the terminal was real and Kalden was real and as long as there was the terminal to trap her, Kalden could find her.

Remembering that Raven would use the terminal she had forced herself to test it and realized for the first time what lay beyond it. They called it a net and it was the net Kalden would use to trap her. Revenge's identity spun through the data networks, careering through nodes and systems, breaking through security protocols with the power of her fear. Everywhere she travelled she found lists, of names, numbers, dates and times, lists which said where everything was supposed to be, lists which would help Kalden to track her. The net was made of light, the only places its tendrils didn't extend were the depths of the city, the slums and ganglands where the sun couldn't penetrate and the lighting burnt out. But the depths of the city were dark and Revenge recoiled from their threat. Racing away from the edge of the net she shot through it again. Everywhere she travelled she closed doors behind her, blocked off junctions, ceased the flow of data. Behind her, systems fell silent, the fear of the dark spurring her on to move faster. The tide of her presence was felt across the city as systems shut down, the inaudible murmur of information slowed and began to stop.

The lights flickered and Raven shivered suddenly, breaking the tension in the hotel room.

'Something's wrong,' she said and the lights went out. The others froze but Raven was a blur of motion, darting towards the window and opening the thick curtains.

'Look,' she said and the others hurried to join her, blundering blindly into objects as they crossed the room.

It was midday and the hotel was on one of the higher levels, so some grey light from the sun gave them a view of the city. But nothing else did. From the depths upwards the lights had gone out, from every walkway and archway, every window in the skyscrapers was black and the darkness was spreading. Further up into the heights lights were still going out. Holo-projections disappeared like ghosts and silence muffled the city.

'It's like the end of the world,' Avalon whispered, staring out at the suddenly strange scene before them.

'Check the vidscreen and the terminal,' Wraith instructed.

'No use,' Raven replied from out of the darkness but Luciel fumbled across the room anyway.

'They're both dead,' he confirmed after a few moments. 'Nothing doing.'

'It has to be a Hex,' Ali exclaimed.

'Unfortunately, yes,' Raven agreed and moved back across the room toward the vidcom. Suddenly the screen lit up with a soft glow and the others could see Raven's pale fingers resting lightly on the screen. 'It's difficult,' she said quietly. 'Everywhere systems are shredding. It's like a virus replicating throughout the net.' Before she could continue the screen sprang to life with an image of Kez, looking scared.

'*Raven!*' he exclaimed. '*What's going on? Everything's stopped working!*'

'Check on Revenge,' Raven instructed.

'*That's what I mean!*' Kez looked frantic. '*It looks like she's had some kind of fit and the monitors aren't working.*'

'Is she still breathing?' Wraith demanded, his body tense with shock.

'*Just about.*' Kez looked at him. '*But I don't know what to do!*'

'Do the best you can,' Raven instructed. 'I'll be with you shortly.' She took her hands from the vidcom and the signal winked out, leaving the unit as dead as before. She was already moving towards the door.

'Wait!' Wraith called after her, moving to catch up.

'Not you,' Raven replied, turning to halt him. 'Revenge didn't know enough to hide what she did. The CPS could already be on their way. Stay here with the others. If I can't stop them, you won't be able to help.'

With that she was gone, the door closing behind her as the others were left in the darkened room.

Across the dark city a pair of needle-like blue eyes stared out through the levels.

'It's her,' he said to himself. 'I'm certain of it.' Turning to the man behind him, his uniform marking him as a senior officer in the security services, his lined skin wrinkled in a rare smile.

'Have your men stand ready,' he ordered. 'Once we've re-initialized the network, your team can track the disturbance to its source. Then it will be your job to apprehend the Hex responsible.'

'A Hex did this?' the officer exclaimed, his surprise betraying him into informality.

'So I suspect,' Dr Kalden replied. 'This incident will persuade the government to give me the resources I need to eliminate them.'

Raven's flitter cut through the chaos of the city like a shark in the depths of the ocean. Thousands of flitters and skimmers clogged the bridges and archways, the loss of the city net depriving them of lights and direction. A few attempted to navigate with only their own lights to guide them but were making slow progress across the complex tangle of bridges. Raven passed them at the flitter's top speed, its lights flashing across the confusion. Without the network to guide her, she was forced to pilot the craft on eyesight and the speed of her reactions alone, trusting to her eidetic memory to furnish her with directions back to the apartment.

One pale hand lay dormant on the console as she used the other to pilot the flitter, keeping track of the situation within the net. It had fragmented, but the powerful computers which held it together had only been wounded by the loss. Slowly they were coming back on line, repairing themselves, ready to launch their own attack. All the broken tendrils of the net led back to one source and as the net was restored that source would become increasingly obvious. Raven's only chance to save Revenge lay in reaching the apartment before the CPS and the console told her that she would be too late. Whispers of information were starting to echo across London again.

If she'd allowed herself more time to consider, Raven

might have decided Revenge and Kez were already lost. But she didn't allow herself the luxury of consideration. Her pride exhorted her to challenge the limits of possibility, and she refused to recognize the possibility of arriving too late. Turning the flitter on its nose she dived through the levels, before sweeping in a curve that brushed the flitter against one of the colossal skyscrapers and skimming past the bridges. The area was still dark but the net was back on line and Raven threw herself out of the flitter as it touched down, leaving the power running. She raced up the stairs to the apartment; the elevators were powered by the network and their lights were off. The door to the apartment was locked and she knocked on it hard.

'Who is it?' Kez's voice was high and frightened.

'Raven.'

The door was opened and she saw the room beyond was dark.

'Here,' Kez said, shutting the door behind her and taking her hand to lead her across the room. 'She collapsed in front of the terminal. I went to find her when the lights went out and . . .'

'She's shorted out the entire city network and the CPS will be here any moment.'

Kez's gasp was silenced by a short harsh scream which suddenly cut off. Raven made her way to the sound. Revenge lay on the floor, curled into the foetal position and whimpering to herself.

'What is it?' Raven demanded. 'Revenge, where are you?'

The whimpering continued, then became words.

'In the dark,' the child whispered and Raven swore under her breath. In under a second the lights came on and Kez could see Raven kneeling on the floor next to

Revenge. The whimpering stopped and the girl's eyes glazed over under the lights as she clung to Raven with skinny arms and legs. As Raven stood, lifting Revenge's slight figure without any difficulty, a siren began to wail in the street, joined by a chorus of others in the distance.

'Close the curtains,' Raven hissed and Kez ran across the room to do it. As he pulled back the heavy drapes he glanced outside and turned to look at Raven.

'There's three Seccie flitters out there!'

'Stay chill,' Raven said softly, shifting Revenge's weight in her arms to reach into her jacket, and produced a pistol.

Nodding silently, Kez started to move towards the door then froze at the sound of footsteps in the corridor.

'*Drop your weapons!*' an amplified voice demanded.

'Come and make me!' Kez snarled back.

'*This is the Security Services,*' the voice boomed. '*You are under arrest. Drop your weapons and come out with your hands up!*'

Raven levelled her pistol at the door, then to Kez's surprise lowered it again. Her eyes were fixed on the door.

'Checkmate,' she whispered as the gas started to roll under the door. Revenge began to cough and Kez ran for the window.

'No use,' Raven told him. 'Strengthened glass.' She lifted Revenge higher, above the clouds of gas. The little girl's lips were blue and she was choking. 'She's dying,' Raven said softly. 'The dosage is too strong.'

'Should we surrender?' Kez asked. Raven shrugged.

'Not much point for me,' she told him. Revenge had lost consciousness and Raven lay her down gently on one of the chairs, sitting on the floor as the gas rolled over them both. 'Goodbye, Kez.'

It was hard to breathe and Kez felt dizzy as he tried to move towards them. He had to crawl the last few inches to take Raven's hand. It was cold but her fingers brushed his lightly as he sank unconscious to the floor.

Wraith paced up and down the hotel suite. The lights had come on again fifteen minutes ago and still there had been no word from Raven. Luciel was scanning the newsfeeds but, while every channel carried the story of the unexpected blackout, there was no clue as to what might have happened to Revenge. Avalon, unwilling to intrude on their private affairs, had offered to leave but remained when Wraith said that Raven's fate concerned her too. All of them knew that without Raven their greatest asset was gone, even though no one was ready to acknowledge it, still hoping that she would return safely. Now Avalon was talking quietly to Ali, listening to the teenager's story of how she had found out she was a Hex. It hadn't taken the megastar long to realize that Ali was jealous of Raven and her feelings of inadequacy had been exacerbated by this current situation.

An exclamation from Luciel had them all clustering around the vidscreen as one of the media channels abruptly changed to a view of their apartment.

'*We're now coming to you live from the source of this afternoon's disturbance,*' the news anchor was saying. '*Half an hour ago SS and CPS operatives surrounded this normal-looking apartment and captured two members of the dangerous terrorist group that threatened the security of the country with their destruction of a CPS facility last year. A third individual was taken directly to Saint Christopher's hospital and pronounced dead on arrival. Although the Security Services have not yet made any official statement it is widely believed that one of the apprehended criminals is the terrorist named Raven who the Prime Minister vowed would be caught.*

'As you can see here, SS officials have closed the crime scene and have apparently brought in additional CPS specialists to study the area. Meanwhile the terrorists are undergoing questioning at a secure facility and the mutant, Raven, is expected to be terminated later this evening. We now go to the studio for an in-depth analysis of these latest events.'

Luciel muted the vidcom and turned to Wraith.

'I'm sorry,' he said and was echoed by Avalon. Wraith looked stricken. There had been no mention of Revenge in the broadcast and he knew what must have been her fate. As for Raven, the guilt seemed more than he could bear. He seemed to hear Ali's voice as if from a great distance away.

'They won't exterminate her.'

'What?' Luciel frowned at her.

'Raven said Dr Kalden never had the opportunity to study a functioning Hex,' Ali reminded them. 'Well, he's got one now, hasn't he? I bet there are a lot of tests he'll want to do.'

'Better if she had died,' Luciel said coldly, voicing the thought the others were thinking.

'But . . .' Ali looked confused. 'Aren't we even going to try to rescue her?'

'How can we?' Wraith said bleakly. 'Without Raven we wouldn't have had a chance last time. What hope do we have without her now?'

Such resignation was untypical of the white-haired ganger and Avalon seemed to realize it as well as any of them.

'We can't decide here,' she said firmly, taking charge of

the shell-shocked group. 'You'd better come back with me.'

'No,' Wraith protested. 'We're a liability.'

'Without Raven you're without resources, right?' Avalon insisted. 'And we have a lot to talk about anyway. Come on – who's going to look for you with me?'

'I think you're right,' Luciel agreed, turning off the vidcom. 'It's not as if we have a lot of other options.'

Avalon's residence was at the top of a skyscraper section on the edge of London. She shared the fifty odd rooms with the other members of Masque but sometimes they didn't see each other for days at a time. As she escorted Wraith, Ali and Luciel into the residence there was no sign of the other band members. Wraith showed no reaction at all to the opulence of their surroundings but Ali and Luciel were wide-eyed. The rooms they passed through were lavishly decorated in deep lush colours; Egyptian artefacts and artworks were scattered across surfaces and elaborate masks hung on the walls.

Avalon took them into an extensive living room and made drinks of a sweet fruit juice.

'I'd offer you alcohol,' she explained. 'But I think you have a lot you need to decide and so do I.' She smiled politely but already she seemed more distant than when they had waited together for news of Raven. 'I'll leave you alone now, if you don't mind. There's a lot I have to think about.'

With that she departed and the two younger members immediately turned to look at Wraith.

'Ali's right,' Luciel began. 'We have to try to save Raven.'

'Of course.' Wraith had recovered something of his composure, his grey eyes no longer looked like shattered glass. 'But it will be difficult.'

'Raven can probably do something towards saving herself,' Ali put in. 'She's told us often enough not to underestimate her.'

'She could be injured.' Wraith looked concerned. 'And the news bulletin indicated that Kez was taken too – that is, if Rachel was the casualty.'

We might be able to get more information on that,' Luciel suggested. 'The Countess has contacts who could find out.'

'And she provided men for the raid on the lab,' Ali added. 'Perhaps we could do that again?'

'There's the building Raven rented from her as well,' Wraith remembered. 'That would be a better place to plan than this. We shouldn't rely on Avalon's generosity, especially now that we are a danger to her.'

'I think we should try to bring Avalon in,' Luciel contradicted, surprised to hear himself take such a stand in planning their future. Now that Raven was absent and Wraith affected so badly, he felt for the first time as if his counsel was needed. But his conviction that he was doing the right thing gave him the courage to make his views felt. 'Avalon could be an asset to us. We're supposed to be trying to fight for the rights of Hexes – we should try to recruit as many people as possible who carry the gene.'

'We don't know how many Hexes there are,' Ali reminded him. 'Or if they'll want to join us.' She, like Luciel, was also experiencing a new freedom to express her opinions and the feeling that she was actually a part of the group.

'We could try to find out,' Luciel insisted. 'And let people know that we exist and might be able to help them.'

'We shouldn't get too hasty,' Wraith warned. 'Right now it's as much as we can do to help ourselves. But getting word to the Countess sounds like a good idea. And I think that we should leave for the new residence as soon as possible.'

'We should rest first,' Ali said. 'And probably eat something. The city's probably still dealing with the effects of the blackout. It might be a good idea to wait until things have calmed down.'

'There must be a Nutromac somewhere here,' Luciel suggested. 'I'm sure Avalon won't mind if we use it.'

Avalon sat on the floor in the middle of her sumptuously appointed bedroom. It, like most of the residence, had been decorated by professionals hired by the band's manager. The four-poster bed and the gold inlaid furniture suited Avalon's idea of the megastar but she always felt a little as if the room belonged to someone else. Despite media adulation she hadn't changed that much from the clubland musician, sharing rooms with a group of other hopefuls waiting for the big chance to prove themselves. She had succeeded but megastardom didn't sit so easily on her shoulders as it did on Elohim's. Or even Cloud's, she thought to herself. Since joining Masque, Cloud Estavisti was becoming a star in his own right and Avalon knew how capably he would deal with it. And on that thought there was a knock on the door.

'Come in,' she called, expecting one of the ill-named terrorists but instead it was Cloud, dressed in holo-weave clothing the same dark blue as his eyes.

'I hope I'm not disturbing you,' he said lightly. 'But you seem to have mislaid some visitors. I found one of them wandering around looking for a Nutromac and directed him to the kitchen.'

'Oh, yes,' Avalon sighed. 'Thank you, Cloud. They are my visitors but I needed some time alone for a second.'

'Shall I leave?' he offered.

Avalon shook her head. 'Perhaps you can give me some advice.'

'If I can,' Cloud said with a thoughtful smile, seating himself on the floor beside her. 'You rarely seem to need advice.'

'Although you give it anyway,' Avalon returned. 'Now I need it.' She sighed again. 'My visitors need help and I feel obliged to provide it. For various reasons I think they have a claim on me. But if I help them I can't stop at basic necessities – I'll need to give up more than that. Probably all of this.' She gestured at the room.

'I see.' Cloud raised an eyebrow. 'Or rather, I don't see. Why do these strangers have that sort of a claim on you? You haven't been doing anything ill-advised, have you? Even if you think it can break your career, something can probably be arranged. I've never heard of a blackmailer that couldn't be bribed one way or another.'

'No,' Avalon said quickly. 'It's nothing like that. But they're . . . they're freedom fighters of a sort, and I believe in their cause.'

'Their cause?' Cloud looked incredulous. 'Avalon, in all the time I've known you, I've thought you had the discipline to survive the occasional insanity of this kind of life, the feeling of power that encourages so many of us to destroy ourselves. But now you're suggesting sacrificing everything you've worked for all your life to help some political terrorists. Even if you do believe in their cause surely you can use your position to help them more than you can as another starving freedom fighter?'

'Then your advice is to abandon them,' Avalon said sharply.

'And to save yourself.' Cloud stood up. 'I'm sorry if it's not the advice you wanted. But they'll drag you down,

Avalon, and us with you if you don't break from them now.' Turning in a whirl of shimmering blue light, he left the room and Avalon looked after him, wondering if he was right.

All three of them ate sparingly of the meal Luciel had dialled from the Nutromac when he eventually found it.

'There's a whole kitchen as well,' he added. 'I didn't think anyone cooked for themselves any more.'

'They probably don't,' Ali told him. 'Although my father and I had a Nutromac we had a kitchen as well and hired people to come and cook for us. Home-cooked food tastes better but it's expensive and anyone who can afford to install a kitchen can usually afford to hire professionals to cook for them.'

'I saw Cloud Estavisti as well,' Luciel told them. 'He doesn't exactly look real, does he? I felt like I was talking to his holo.'

'He's very talented,' Ali said defensively. 'Next to Avalon he's the most famous member of Masque.'

'It's light years away from the kind of life we're leading,' Luciel replied. 'It's hard to believe Avalon is one of us.'

'Raven didn't seem to think so,' Ali reminded him. You heard what she said – she didn't want to teach us but she wanted to teach Avalon.'

'Raven said she was committed to teaching you,' Wraith corrected her. 'And that was a large concession for her to make. She's always preferred to work alone. If she felt a special sympathy for Avalon it might well have been because she's shared something of Raven's experience, growing up knowing she was under sentence of death.'

Ali fell silent and Luciel tried to break the tension.

'Do you think Raven would like it here?' he asked from where he stood at the window looking down at the city. 'She seems comfortable wherever she is.'

'I don't think Raven cares where she is,' Wraith replied. 'Except now.'

Luciel nodded and began to move away from the window. Suddenly he froze, then moved back quickly and silently.

'Wraith,' he said urgently. 'There are a lot of Seccie flitters out there all of a sudden.'

'You don't think Avalon would have—' Ali began but was cut off by Wraith.

'I'm trying not to think it,' he said, taking his laser pistol out. To Ali's surprise Luciel produced his own. As he was checking it over the door opened and both of them turned to face it. Avalon blanched as she found herself staring down the barrel of a gun.

'What's going on?' she demanded.

'There are armed flitters out there with Seccie ID,' Wraith told her.

'Oh no.' Avalon ran over to the window and looked out. 'I promise I didn't call them,' she said quickly, realizing their probable thoughts.

'How did they find us?' Luciel asked. 'No one else knew we were here.'

'Cloud!' Avalon exclaimed, her shock obvious to the rest of them. 'I can't believe he'd do this.'

'We'd better find him,' Wraith said.

6
Virtue and Form

The slim ethereal figure of Cloud Estavisti confronted the Hex grouping in Masque's opulent residence. Alone and unarmed he had the best defence against them. Wraith couldn't have shot him, even if he felt the dancer deserved it.

'Cloud, how could you?' Avalon's voice was hopelessly confused.

'You couldn't do it yourself,' Cloud told her. 'And it needed to be done. I told the Security Services you were being held hostage. You won't be connected with them.'

'I am connected to them,' Avalon raged at him. 'And you've forced me to admit it. I can't risk the SS arresting me any more than they can. If I do, I'm in danger of my life.' She turned to Wraith. 'You have to leave now, if you still can. Will you take me with you?'

'Of course,' the ganger said courteously.

'Avalon, this is unwise,' Cloud protested but she rounded on him, violet eyes blazing.

'Betrayer,' she flung at him. 'I can trust strangers better than you. I suppose you'd have sold me out to the CPS too if you'd known what I was.' Turning her back on him, she stalked across the room. 'There are flitters on the upper level,' she announced. 'We can probably outrun them for a while.'

'Is there anything you'd like to take with you?' Wraith

asked, also turning his back on Cloud. Luciel moved to follow them and only Ali hung back. Cloud's expression was unreadable and for a moment he reminded her of Raven. Then he noticed her standing there and looked derisively at her.

'Go on, then,' he said. 'You don't want to be left behind, do you?'

'No, I don't,' she said angrily and turned to catch up with the others, thinking that Wraith or Luciel should have at least incapacitated him to prevent him from further mischief.

Ali caught up with the others on the roof. Avalon had somewhere acquired an electric guitar which she wore slung over one shoulder. The flitter bay was full with luxury craft and Avalon had led them to a sleek black vehicle which looked designed for speed.

'I'll pilot,' Luciel volunteered. 'Wraith, can you hold them off with your pistol when we go out?'

'I can attempt it,' the ganger said wryly. 'Give your pistol to Ali.'

'There's no point,' Ali said. 'It's not as if I can use it.'

'I can,' Avalon interjected, to their surprise. 'Give it to me.' She took the weapon with a surprising ease and smiled at their expressions. 'Not everyone is content to rely on the protection of bodyguards,' she explained. 'Besides, I grew up in the slums.'

Ali climbed into the back, beside the singer, and watched as Luciel operated the controls to the bay door and began to pilot the flitter out. Wraith and Avalon slid down their windows and sighted down their pistols, waiting for the first sign of pursuit.

Alaric watched the news item in silence. Other members of Anglecynn looked up expectantly when he turned off the battered vidcom. Since he had issued instructions that everyone should remain at Dragon's Nest, almost the entire group was there. Sixty people, of which only five including himself were founding members and only another fifteen were veterans of over two years.

'It looks like that's it,' Alaric told them. 'I had hoped to discuss the possibility of sharing some resources with the Hex group but it seems the idea comes too late.'

'Why not discuss it anyway?' Geraint asked. Next to Alaric he was the oldest member of the group and to anyone else the remark would have constituted an order.

'It's possible not all of them were captured,' Jordan added.

'Well, what would be general feelings on forming an alliance with the rebel Hexes?' Alaric asked, throwing the question open.

'As long as they're against the EF, I'm for them,' Maggie announced, drawing noises of support from some of the others.

'Hell, they've got even more reason than us to be against it,' one of the younger members added. 'Stands to reason they'll want to get rid of the extermination laws.'

'I don't know.' Geraint looked uncertain. 'We don't know anything about the Hex powers. I've heard them called witches and demons. I think we ought to know what we're getting into before we consider involving ourselves with them.'

'Excuse me?' To Alaric's surprise Daniel Hammond was signalling for attention and he waved the others silent for a moment. 'Thank you,' Daniel said nervously. 'I know I'm a new member but I think you ought to know I once knew someone who I think could be part of their group. She was one of my sister's friends, a bit spoilt and a little vain but she certainly wasn't any kind of demon. I don't think she could have even known she was a Hex and she must have been terrified when they took her away. I don't know how she escaped. But I'm glad she did.'

'Daniel's right,' Jordan agreed. 'The legalized extermination of the Hexes is one of the laws we should be fighting. Otherwise we sanction the government-authorized murder of children with no other fault than a genetic anomaly they couldn't help having.'

The meeting broke up almost immediately into smaller discussions as everyone attempted to debate the idea at once. None of the veterans intervened while the discussion went on, taking part in it equally enthusiastically. But after about fifteen minutes, Alaric glanced at Geraint, who nodded.

'I think we ought to take this to a vote,' Geraint suggested, his voice effectively silencing the others. 'How many are in favour of making some contact with what might remain of this group, with a view to further discussion?'

About half the room raised their hands immediately and were followed after a few moments by most of the others.

'Would those opposed like to speak?' Alaric asked and the first of the dissenters stepped forward. As he began to outline his arguments, Jordan leaned forward and squeezed Alaric's hand.

'I think it's carried,' she said in an undertone. 'There's already a majority in favour.'

'Let's hope when we've decided there's still someone left to contact,' Alaric replied.

Shots ricocheted from the side of the flitter and it lurched alarmingly as Luciel attempted to swing it away from the pursuit. Leaning dangerously out of her window, Avalon fired off a couple of blasts at random and leant in again as Luciel swung the craft round, aiming for a space down to the next level. Wraith leant out of his window, firing more deliberately, and Ali called:

'They're falling back!'

'Not far enough,' Luciel replied, diving down a level and flipping the light vehicle round a bridge support.

A fusillade of shots confirmed his words as the Seccie flitters continued the chase, fanning out in an attempt to encircle them. Luciel accelerated again, swearing to himself.

'How do I lose them?' he exclaimed involuntarily.

'Head for the ganglands, then pull off through the slums and come back again,' Wraith instructed. 'If you have to, go right into the depths, but watch out, there's no lighting at all down there and a lot of the arches have fallen.' He leant out through the window and fired again, holding back the Seccies as Luciel attempted to get a lead on them, piloting the flitter in a crazy spin across the level. Avalon was firing as well but few of her shots hit.

'It's not quite like my training,' she excused herself.

'You don't need to shoot to kill,' Wraith replied. 'Just scare them a little, make them fall back.'

'I'm trying,' Avalon assured him, then spun to look at him as the ganger gave an odd curse.

Wraith collapsed back in his seat and Ali saw blood staining his jacket.

'What happened?' she asked, her voice shrill with alarm.

'Dropped the pistol, dammit,' Wraith said succinctly. 'Took a hit in my right arm.'

'How bad is it?' Ali asked, desperately trying to remember the first aid course she'd taken at school.

'I've taken worse,' Wraith replied raggedly. 'But it's bad timing.'

'Maybe not that bad,' Luciel said with relief. 'We're pulling ahead.'

The flitter shot through the levels, pursued by the Seccie swarm; but as the greasy lights of gangland drew near, Luciel executed a fast turn which sent their flitter spinning in a dive down the levels, before yanking the craft back up with a jolt. They swung past a building that loomed alarmingly close, then sped back up through the levels again.

'Can you see them?' Luciel demanded and Ali clung on to her seat as she attempted to look back.

'Not any more,' she replied and Luciel immediately cut the speed, sending the flitter cruising more comfortably through the more respectable slums.

'They'll have our description,' Wraith warned.

'Next level down we'll dump the flitter then,' Luciel replied. 'Once we've stolen another we should be relatively safe.'

It was an anxious ride that seemed excruciatingly slow to all of them until Luciel spotted an alternative craft and pulled in. The others waited inside while he walked casually towards it and attempted to disable the lock. A few years ago he wouldn't have had any idea how to pick a lock but, since customizing the flitter he'd worked on with Kez, he'd learnt a few things. After five minutes that felt like an eternity he cracked it open and turned to signal the others. They hurried over to the new vehicle, Ali supporting Wraith, who looked even more pale than usual. Once they were inside, Luciel got the flitter moving at a fast but just legal speed and they headed back towards gangland.

'Once we get to the building we can see about fixing

you up,' he told Wraith. 'I just hope Raven managed to include some medical supplies in that inventory of hers.'

The room was cold and grey. A dim light glowed from a panel high above, shining into Kez's eyes as he awoke. He felt nauseous and the first breath he drew made him cough. Dragging himself roughly upright he saw for the first time the other figure in the room. Raven lay against the wall, looking like a broken doll, her face white and still. Crawling towards her, still shaken by hacking coughs, Kez reached for her wrist and tried to feel a pulse. After a few bleak seconds he found it, fluttering lightly under Raven's almost translucently pale skin. Pulling himself up again to sit next to her, Kez took Raven's shoulders and shook them lightly.

'Raven,' he whispered, his voice rough and hoarse. 'Wake up!'

The older girl stirred slightly, then opened ebony eyes and began to cough. He helped her sit up and she leant back against the wall of their cell as she tried to stop herself choking. Finally she stopped and, catching her breath, began to look at their surroundings.

'Are you all right?' Kez asked anxiously.

'More or less,' Raven replied. She looked around the room again before saying to herself. 'And here I am again.'

'You've been here before?'

'Hardly,' Raven replied. 'But places like this.' Stretching out her legs to make herself more comfortable on the cold floor, she continued: 'Back in Denver, I grew up in an asylum blockhouse. A standard punishment was locking us in a room something like this one.'

'What did you do?' Kez asked.

'Nothing,' Raven replied. 'Waited.' She shrugged. 'I'm sure this cell is well enough designed that I couldn't get out of it by any conventional means and nothing unconventional comes to mind right now. So we wait and sooner or later someone will turn up and we'll find out a little more.'

'They will?'

'Sooner or later,' Raven confirmed. 'Either to question us or torture us or just stand there and laugh.'

'That doesn't sound too good,' Kez said uneasily.

'It isn't too good,' Raven replied. 'Being dead might be a better option but that didn't happen, so we wait.'

'Don't you have anything that might help?' Kez asked hopefully.

'If there was a lock I could probably pick it,' Raven told him. 'But there isn't one on this side.'

'Aren't you scared?'

'It wouldn't be productive.' Raven's eyes met his seriously. 'Fear isn't going to help us get out of here.'

When the flitter touched down in front of the gangland building everyone was tense with nerves. Ali helped Wraith out of the flitter and Luciel led them towards the building. As they approached the main entrance Luciel paused, looking at the blue and gold Snake emblem that was slashed across the door.

'This wasn't here before,' he said warningly. Cautiously he tried to open it. 'It's locked.'

'Can you open it?' Avalon asked.

'I think so,' Luciel replied. 'Unless Raven's been playing with it, in which case I don't have a chance.'

Ali helped Wraith to the side of the building so he could lean against it and slumped down at his feet. She felt grimy and bruised from the ride and almost impossibly tired. Luciel was fiddling with the lock while Avalon covered them with his pistol.

'This might be it,' he said after a few minutes.

'Wait a second.' Avalon put her hand over his, gesturing for silence. 'Can you hear something?'

The others listened. Traffic noises filtered down from the upper levels but there was nothing nearby.

'Inside the building,' Avalon insisted. She frowned, her head half tilted to catch the faint noise, then stepped back, waving the others off. 'Someone's coming,' she whispered.

Silently, Luciel took the pistol from her and levelled it at the door. Still leaning against the wall, Wraith reached into his jacket and revealed a lethal-looking knife and held it out towards Avalon. Then he pushed himself upright and took a fighting stance. Fumbling in the garbage Ali grabbed hold of a short metal pole, broken off from some piece of machinery, and got to her feet. Then the door opened and Luciel found himself pointing a pistol at a man with a machine gun.

'Chill, kid!' Jeeva said quickly. 'Ain't no call to be shooting.'

Ali almost collapsed with relief and tried to disguise it by taking Wraith's arm as he also sagged against the wall.

'Jeeva!' Luciel said with relief. 'Thank God. We need help.'

'Looks like it,' Jeeva agreed, slinging his gun and moving to help support Wraith into the building. 'What's going down?'

'Raven's been caught, and Kez,' Luciel explained. 'Wraith was shot while we were escaping from the Seccies.'

'I scan.' Jeeva set Wraith down on an empty crate in the main room and hurried to lock and then bar the door.

Crossing the room he opened one of the doors leading up to a set of stairs and called up it: 'Hey, Finn! Get down here!'

Booted feet rang on the stairway and Finn appeared in the entrance hall. He went immediately to Wraith and motioned the others aside so he could inspect the injury.

'Bullet wound,' he said to himself. 'Not a blaster. It'll have to be taken out.' He looked round the group and focused on Ali. 'Is anything major going to go down in the next few minutes or can we have this taken care of properly?'

'I think so,' Ali replied nervously, looking to the others for reassurance.

'Then in that case we'll take him upstairs,' Finn decided. 'Jeeva, get on the com to the Countess. Tell her we need a medic and probably more back-up. Where's Raven?'

'Captured,' Luciel told him. 'Kez as well.'

'Tell her that too,' Finn instructed. 'And get her to send over some more technicians – we'll need to get this place up and running fast. You scan?'

'Understood,' Jeeva said briefly and left the room at an easy loping run.

'We'd best get Wraith upstairs,' Finn continued. 'Help me carry him,' he addressed Luciel. 'You two get up to the control room and start getting stuff uncrated.'

Ali and Avalon glanced at each other as Finn lifted Wraith into a standing position.

'Thank you,' he said faintly. 'I appreciate this.'

'Don't sweat it,' Finn replied. 'Raven hired us to get this place operational, you've just made it a bit more urgent, that's all.' Hoisting Wraith up between him and Luciel he started to head back towards the stairs.

'Wait a moment,' Avalon called after him.

‘What?’ Finn didn’t look back.

‘Where’s the control room?’

‘Second door along, up the stairs, straight ahead there’s a room full of crates. That’s it.’

With that he disappeared up the stairwell and Ali and Avalon were left alone.

‘I suppose we go upstairs then,’ Avalon said ruefully. ‘Though I’m not sure what we’re supposed to be doing.’

‘Neither am I,’ Ali admitted. ‘Maybe we’ll find out when we get there.’

The door opened so smoothly that Kez didn’t notice the difference until a shadow fell over his face. Looking up quickly he saw the door blocked by four uniformed men. As they spread out and took guard positions around the room a fifth entered. Unlike the others he was elderly, his hair white with age and his face lined. But his blue eyes were bright as he entered the room, closing the door carefully behind him and coming to face the two prisoners.

‘This is an unexpected pleasure,’ he said pleasantly. ‘I’m not certain of your identity, young man, but you must be Raven – or do you prefer Miss Raven?’

‘Just Raven,’ the girl replied, still seated on the floor, with Kez crouched uneasily beside her.

‘Raven,’ Kalden confirmed. ‘Well, my dear, it looks as if you’ve made an unfortunate mistake.’

‘It does appear that way,’ Raven agreed. ‘But you’d be wrong to think so.’

‘Then you planned to find yourself here,’ Kalden suggested with an edge of sarcasm.

‘Not exactly, but I’m finding the experience instructive.’

‘Then we shall endeavour to provide you with further opportunities for your education,’ Kalden replied coldly. ‘I trust you will find them equally instructive.’

'I hope so.' Raven stretched out her legs and looked up at the scientist with a dispassionate interest. 'But I'm often disappointed. If I were you I'd have us both executed now.'

'I'm sure you would, Miss.' Kalden smiled, showing his teeth. 'But I am not so foolish as that. I expect to learn a lot from you.' Turning on his heel he opened the door again and the guards moved to cover him as they exited the room. Less than a minute later the door swung shut again, sealing with a dull clang.

'No one ever takes what I say at face value,' Raven reflected. 'Perhaps we should try and get some sleep. From the sound of it Kalden is planning a busy schedule for us.' She shifted position to lie flat on her back on the smooth floor.

'Raven?' Kez asked, attempting to compose himself similarly.

'Yes?'

'Did you mean that? About executing us?'

Raven laughed quietly.

'Does it matter?' she asked. 'He won't do it.'

'But would you?'

'Of course,' Raven replied. 'If a threat exists, it should be removed immediately and effectively. If a threat does not exist, any action taken to circumvent it is futile. Now go to sleep.'

Raven's credit with the Countess was obviously better than the others had imagined because in less than an hour the fixer had sent over five of her guards and two technicians as well as a street doctor whose credentials Finn vouched for. While he was attending to Wraith's arm, Finn took the technical experts to the control room where Ali and Avalon had successfully uncrated all the equipment and had stacked it up around the room. Neither of them had understood much of it. There were banks of panels and monitor screens as well as a lot of seemingly random electrical components and power cabling. But the technicians, a man and a woman who introduced themselves as Cy and Selda, seemed to know exactly what was intended.

'Monster of a security system,' Cy commented, looking around the room at the assorted components. 'Let's start getting it set up.' Selda grabbed a coil of the cabling and Ali and Avalon found themselves relegated to a corner of the room as the technicians started wiring parts together. Avalon watched them intently but after a while Ali slipped away and went to find Wraith. He was asleep on a pile of blankets in a suite of empty rooms, with Luciel watching over him.

'Hi,' Ali said softly as she came in and sat on the floor beside them. 'How is he?'

'Doctor said he'd cracked the bone and lost a lot of blood but he should heal OK if he's easy on it. That's how come the bandaging. He'll need a sling once he gets up.'

'What do we do without him?' Ali asked nervously.

'I don't know.' Luciel shook his head. 'But we'll have to try.' He grinned ruefully. 'Technically you should be in charge now.'

'Why me?' Ali looked alarmed.

'Apart from Kez, you've known Raven and Wraith the longest,' Luciel explained. 'You know what they'd do better than me.'

'I'm not sure about that,' Ali contradicted. 'And even if I did, what good does it do to say that Raven would hack some secure system and Wraith would storm it with guns blazing? I can't do any of that.'

'So we'll have to think of something else,' Luciel replied. 'Maybe Avalon can help.'

'Maybe.' Ali looked doubtful.

'By the way,' Luciel added, 'we might have something to go on. The Countess passed on a message from some group who want to open negotiations with us. Says they're called Anglecynn and they're anti the European Federation.'

'What do they want with us?' Ali asked.

'No idea.' Luciel looked blank. 'The implication was that we have to start negotiations before we can find out.'

Kez was asleep and Raven listened thoughtfully to the even sound of his breathing. She suspected the only reason he was still alive was that Kalden thought he might be a Hex. Revenge was almost certainly dead already.

Laying her palm flat on the floor she concentrated. Somewhere out there the net still existed, even with no apparent way to reach it. But it was far away and she couldn't even sense its presence. She let her mind go blank, reaching out as far as she could. There. A flicker of familiarity. A random datastream intersecting momentarily with her consciousness. She reached for it and lost it. Reached out again and found nothing. But it was there. She stared up at the ceiling. She would need to conserve her energies and she doubted that the task ahead would be easy. But she had no intention of surrendering herself to Kalden's experiments.

She wasn't a child any longer. Hadn't been a child since she'd escaped from the asylum and forced the use of her abilities. But that night while she slept Raven dreamed of being alone in the city and everywhere she went the streets were silent.

7

A Fearful Madness

Ali awakened from an uneasy doze as someone shook her by the shoulder. Sitting up quickly, her nerves still on edge since the blackout, she looked up to see Cy, the male technician, taking a hasty step back.

'Didn't mean to startle you, Miss,' he said politely. 'I just came to tell you that your system's up and running and you might want to test it out.'

'Oh.' Ali got out of the battered chair she'd been sleeping in and stood up.

The room she'd been in was unchanged but, as they walked towards the control centre, she could see the corridor had changed. The battered wall panels had been removed and replaced by a smooth black surface which gleamed slightly with a dark red light. As they entered the control room she could see that the changes extended much further. Every wall was covered with vidscreens, large and small, and a semi-circular bank of computer terminals commanded the centre of the room. Avalon, Luciel and Selda were standing in the centre of the semi-circle, looking at a bank of screens showing different vidcam images.

'The cams form a sphere around the perimeter of the immediate area of the building,' Selda was explaining. 'And the others are in the building itself.' Seeing Ali, she turned to include her in the explanation. 'All three stairways and the approach corridors to the control room are force shielded and the staircases have hidden explosives as well.'

Ali took a seat in the middle of the control bank as Selda and Cy continued to explain the system to them. Avalon was listening intently and Luciel even asked a few questions but Ali found most of the technical descriptions went over her head. This was what they needed Raven for, she thought to herself. The teenage hacker had designed this security system herself and the rest of them would be lucky if they could understand it well enough to use it. Ali found Raven difficult to get on with but she admitted to herself that the group needed her more than they'd ever needed Ali. Once the technicians had finished their explanation and left, Ali turned to look at the others.

Avalon was frowning as she studied the terminals, her lips moving silently as she repeated some of the instructions they'd been given.

'I didn't catch most of that,' Ali admitted. 'This is really Raven's system.'

'I know,' Luciel sighed. 'The computer system doesn't even have basic security protocols yet. Raven must have been planning to do all that herself.' He looked hopefully at Avalon. 'How much did you understand?'

'Not enough, I suspect,' she said seriously. 'But at least we have a system now, even if we don't understand it properly. That's better than nothing at all.'

'You're right,' Luciel agreed. 'So what do we do next?'

'Is Wraith still asleep?' Ali asked anxiously.

'Looks like it,' Luciel replied. 'The doc gave him some tranqs when he left and they seem to have knocked him out.'

'Perhaps we could try and make this place more

habitable,' Avalon suggested. 'Right now Wraith doesn't even have a bed.'

'Raven would probably go on a shopping spree,' Ali told her. 'She likes to be comfortable.'

'Let's borrow the large flitter Finn was using earlier,' Luciel said. 'We can go and pick up some furniture and try and make Wraith more comfortable.'

'Is it safe?' Ali asked.

'Take Finn with you for protection,' Avalon said. 'He looks as if he can take care of himself.'

'OK.' Luciel was heading for the door when he thought of something and turned back. 'Thanks for all your help, Avalon. I'm sorry we seem to be causing you so much trouble. I don't think Raven meant all this to affect you.'

'Don't worry too much about it,' Avalon told him. 'This is Cloud's fault more than yours. If it wasn't for him Wraith wouldn't be out of action now when you need him.'

The group of scientists were checking the equipment for the third time, quietly murmuring their results to each other so as not to disturb the trio who observed them. Dr Kalden wore an annoyed expression as he considered the makeshift laboratory.

'The facilities are highly inadequate,' he complained to his companions. 'This subject could represent an important breakthrough for my work and I need specialized equipment to study her. I need more people, more resources and a proper laboratory to work in instead of this basement.'

'I appreciate your concerns, Doctor,' Adam Hammond replied. The Security Minister looked just as exasperated as Dr Kalden. 'But in the circumstances I consider the Security Services have been more than reasonable.' He nodded towards the third man who as yet had said nothing. 'Governor Alverstead has informed me that the European Federation considers your experiments a matter of state secrecy. Therefore I cannot allow you any more assistants than those who have already been involved in this project. My people are working on supplying the equipment you've requested but that much specialized technology cannot be provided immediately. As for the location: this building is the best maximum security facility there is in this city. The subject is considered a dangerous terrorist with unknown abilities. I cannot allow you to remove her from this location especially since she was directly responsible for the escape of test subjects from the facility which was under your sole control.'

'An attack that occurred at a time when the government was refusing me additional funding on the grounds that my project served no useful purpose!' Kalden exclaimed angrily. 'Now I've been proved right! The girl does have abilities which would be of use to the Federation and to your Security Services, Mr Hammond. But still I'm being denied the resources I need to continue.'

'Dr Kalden, Minister.' Charles Alverstead's voice cut smoothly through the argument. 'The Federation Council appreciates the effort you gentlemen have put in to the work of my agency.' The Governor of the CPS turned to consider the scientists flocked around the room. 'This equipment may be far less than you deserve, Doctor. But I am certain a scientist of your calibre will obtain valuable results from it nonetheless. Equally I feel certain that the Minister's security precautions are necessary measures even if they do hamper the experimentation.' Smiling urbanely at both of them he paused to consider his wrist chronometer. 'Since other duties call me away and it appears your team have completed their tests, Dr Kalden, I will leave matters in your capable hands. Please contact me once you have some results from the subject.'

Raven had been giving Kez a history lesson when the guards arrived. Since their cell was certain to be monitored, they couldn't discuss anything that might compromise the others. But there was nothing to do except talk. Raven had attempted to take advantage of the opportunity and the occasion had come out of a question Kez had asked about Wraith's politics. Raven had found herself explaining the structure of the European Federation to him, something Kez had never given any attention to during his childhood on the streets.

'How come you know this stuff anyway?' Kez asked her, interrupting her explanation of Federation law. 'You always say politics is a waste of time.'

'There's no need to be ignorant,' Raven replied. 'Even if intervening in the political situation is futile, it's to our advantage to understand the world we live in.' She smiled wryly. 'But the reason I know this is the same for most hackers. In order to find the right computer system to break into, you need to know who controls it. It's a waste of energy to spend time and effort cracking a computer that doesn't have the information you want because it's the responsibility of a different agency.' She laughed quietly as Kez looked up warningly at the ceiling, which probably concealed the monitors.

'Kez, considering I'm under sentence of death for suspected mutation and due to be experimented on at any time, it's not going to make much difference if the CPS know I worked as a hacker.'

'I guess not,' Kez admitted and they returned to the lesson.

Ten minutes later the guards arrived, pointing their stun guns warningly at the prisoners as they ordered Raven to get up.

'Where are you taking her?' Kez demanded, trying to stand up as well.

'No questions,' one of the guards said roughly, pushing him back down as two of the others took Raven's arms.

She frowned warningly at Kez as they led her out of the cell and he subsided, watching impotently as the door closed behind her.

Raven let the guards march her down the corridor. It was blank and featureless, only a few heavy doors along the way giving an indication of the building's function. Other cells, she speculated, and wondered if they also held prisoners. Her fingers twitched in the wristcuffs the guards had put on her. Somewhere beyond the walls of this corridor was a computer system. The only problem was reaching it. Her mind worked on the problem as they marched her down the corridor and into a large windowless room. White-coated scientists were making adjustments to what looked like a hospital diagnostic bed surrounded by a bank of machinery. As she was brought into the room, Dr Kalden turned to give her a shark-like smile.

'I see Raven has arrived,' he said cheerfully. 'So pleased you could join us.' Raven ignored him and Kalden smiled even more broadly before ordering the guards to strap her onto the bed. Raven allowed them to do so, noticing that Kalden was amused by her cooperation, thinking her numb with fear. She had to clamp down on her emotions to keep from grinning with excitement.

Stupid, ignorant and unimaginative men, she thought to herself. *Surround me with the most sophisticated technology available and you think you're safe because there's no computer terminal in this room.*

She stared blankly up at the ceiling as they attached wires and electrodes to her skin, wiring her up to the machines that surrounded the bed.

'Turn the test equipment on,' Dr Kalden ordered and Raven's body convulsed as electrical impulses ripped through her mind.

The pain was incredible. She'd read about this experiment in Kalden's files. The equipment was supposed to provide a map of her brain by recording her synaptic responses to different energy signals. She'd laughed at it at the time, amused by the way Kalden seemed to think this sort of testing would help him understand the working of the Hex abilities. Now it wasn't so amusing as pain tore through her body with each new signal.

Ignore it, she ordered herself. She forced herself not to remember that it was equipment like this that had left Rachel a shred of her former self. Instead she concentrated on the machines. In a universe the scientists were unable to comprehend, the equipment was sending messages all the time, chittering its results to itself. Raven reached out with her mind.

> **there!** < Behind the chatter of the equipment was a silent force, empty of words, a river of power flowing towards her. She reached out for it. Power cabling, piping energy to Kalden's test equipment.

> **and beyond . . .** < She reached further, nerves screaming in agony as she attempted to ignore the pain. The power cables thrummed with a constant force, providing the city with the power it needed, running into every building, every aspect of city life, endlessly supplying energy. She let her mind be carried with a wash of energy, taking her further and further away from her suffering body.

> almost < She felt it at the edge of her perceptions, the link to the net. The power lines carried her towards it but too slowly. Suddenly there was nothing and the cessation of the pain brought her back to her body as she realized the equipment had been turned off.

'What happened?' Kalden demanded, turning dials on the test equipment.

'I've no idea, sir,' one of the scientists replied nervously. 'It just stopped giving results. All we've got for the last three minutes is static.'

Kalden looked suspiciously at Raven but the girl had collapsed back on the bed, her face grey with pain as she attempted to catch her breath. Kalden knew from experience how the equipment affected his subjects. He could have designed it to be less traumatic for them but he considered that the fear of torture kept them under control. It seemed to have done the same for Raven and he rejected the momentary fear that she could have caused the equipment failure.

'Take her back to the cell,' he ordered the guards. 'We'll need to check this over before we can perform any more tests.'

Raven was still gasping for breath. But at least the link had revealed where she was being held: the EF Consulate.

Wraith woke up to find himself in unfamiliar surroundings. Someone had moved him while he slept, the drugs the Countess's medic had given him preventing him from waking up. Sitting up in bed he looked around the room. It wasn't elaborately furnished but a thick carpet now covered the floor and simple but attractive furniture was scattered around the room. Getting out of bed he arranged the cloth he found waiting for him to form a sling for his injured arm. Then he left the room and began to explore. He was amazed at the changes that had taken place in just a few short hours. All the rooms in this part of the building had been furnished. The layout was similar to the design of the apartment they'd been living in. But, instead of the heavy crimson and russet colours that Raven favoured, the furnishings were in softer greens and blues. One undecorated corridor drew his attention. The black shielding gave him an idea of its purpose and he wasn't entirely surprised to find it led to a control room, although the scale of the equipment inside astonished him.

Finn and Avalon were inside, seated at a semi-circular bank of terminals. The angle of the door prevented them from seeing him and they were evidently absorbed in conversation.

'I didn't realize how much I relied on Cloud until he betrayed us,' Avalon was saying. 'I never realized I trusted him until I trusted him too much.'

'If you run with a gang you have to trust your brothers,' Finn replied. 'But even then you make mistakes. You're not to blame.'

'And I'm very grateful to you,' Wraith added, coming to join them. Avalon smiled but Finn shook his head in annoyance.

'Hidden cams all through this place and we didn't even see you coming, Wraith. We've got to get more people up here to monitor that kind of thing.'

'We?' Wraith asked, taking a seat beside them. 'Are you joining us, Finn?'

'Don't get excited,' Finn replied. 'The Countess made a deal with Raven to supply support for this place until it's working and at the moment that support is me. But when it's done, the Snakes are gone. Otherwise you might starting getting ideas and take my brothers on another schizo rescue mission.'

'Raven's still a prisoner,' Avalon reminded him and Finn shrugged.

'The way I see it, Raven can probably rescue herself. She's an electric hacker and a Hex. Whoever's holding her won't know what hit them.' He grinned suddenly. 'But if you do get round to breaking her out I might come along to see if there's anyone left for you to fight.'

Wraith didn't stay talking for long. Excusing himself he went to find Ali and Luciel. As he continued to explore the building he tried to take comfort in Finn's belief that Raven would be all right. Even though she had proved herself self-sufficient in the past the image of Revenge haunted him. Whenever he thought of Raven being held prisoner he was almost overcome by the fear that he would find her, as he had found Revenge, destroyed by Dr Kalden's horrific experimentation.

Kez rushed to Raven's side as the guards dropped her on the floor. Blood trickled from her mouth where she'd bitten her lip, and her face was grey and lifeless. As the door closed behind the guards he checked her frantically. She didn't seem to be breathing. Taking her wrist, he tried to find a pulse, cursing himself for not knowing more first aid. A dry rasp startled him as Raven suddenly breathed and he almost collapsed with relief.

'Stop crying and help me sit up,' Raven said faintly. 'I'm not dead yet.'

Flushing with embarrassment Kez helped her sit and lean back against the wall.

'What happened?' he asked her. 'I thought they'd killed you.'

'They didn't even complete their first batch of tests,' Raven told him. 'That man is a sadist. I'm going to positively enjoy watching him die.'

'Watching who die?' Kez asked, startled.

'Dr Kalden, of course,' Raven replied, with an edge of annoyance despite her weakness. 'Unless you know of any other sadistic experimenters who require fate's immediate attention.'

'But how will Kalden die?' Kez asked. 'He's almost killed you already.'

'No he hasn't.' Raven frowned. 'I'm just not used to being wired up to a live electric current. And Kalden is doomed whether he knows it or not. There's a significant danger involved in experimenting on people whose abilities you don't understand. Now leave me alone, I need to think.'

Raven closed her eyes and Kez moved away. Although Raven still sounded confident, her appearance worried him. He was also annoyed with Raven. If Wraith had been caught, he would have been a more considerate companion. Raven seemed annoyed by his concern for her and, even though he was sure she was planning something, she kept her own counsel. He also didn't understand why he was being held here. At first he'd thought it was because Dr Kalden thought he was a Hex. But no one had attempted to run any tests on him. He caught his breath as an unnerving thought occurred to him.

'What is it?' Raven asked irritably. Kez blanched at her tone but he couldn't keep silent.

'I just thought,' he said haltingly. 'Maybe they're keeping me here because they think they can use me to get to you. They could torture me to get me to tell them about you.'

'Or to persuade me to help them to save your life,' Raven added. 'It had occurred to me.'

Kez took a deep breath, embarrassed by what he was going to admit.

'I don't know if I can handle torture,' he said. 'It scares me.'

'That's the point of it,' Raven replied unemotionally. Then she gave a half-smile. 'Don't worry about protecting me, Kez. Or the others. Tell them whatever you want.'

'I don't want to tell them anything!' Kez protested. 'I owe you.'

'No you don't.' Raven looked surprised. 'Why would you think that?'

'Because if it wasn't for you I'd still be on the streets!' Kez exclaimed. 'Of course I owe you.'

Raven looked at him silently for a moment. Some colour was returning to her face and she regarded him seriously.

'No, you don't owe me,' she said quietly. 'Since meeting us your life has been in danger almost constantly. Even the penalties for helping a Hex are high. Now you're in greater danger than you've ever been before. There's no reason to think you owe me anything.'

Kez thought for a while before answering. Then he said slowly, 'You gave me something to do with my life. Don't I owe you for that?'

'Maybe,' Raven said thoughtfully. 'Obligations are a decision you have to make for yourself. However, I'd rather you didn't try to risk your life for me.'

'You risked yours,' Kez insisted. 'When you came back to the apartment.'

'I know,' Raven said. 'It was unwise. Especially since I didn't succeed.'

'Why did you come then?' Kez asked.

'I don't know.' Raven looked annoyed. 'Sometimes I don't understand myself.'

'Sometimes no one else does either,' Kez replied.

'At the moment that's probably to our advantage,'

Raven reminded him. Then, to his surprise, she grinned fiercely. 'Dr Kalden has a lot to learn,' she said.

Wraith, Ali and Luciel had been discussing the message from Anglecynn. Although the two younger members of the group had attempted to sort out the arrangements for the base they were still uncertain about what to do next. Rescuing Raven and Kez was the important thing but, with no way of knowing where they were being held, it seemed almost impossible to achieve.

'Perhaps this group could help us?' Luciel suggested. 'They probably have resources we could use.'

'They're terrorists,' Ali objected. 'And we don't know anything about them.'

'The government considers us terrorists,' Wraith reminded her.

'And Raven told us something about them,' Luciel added.

'She said they were naive amateurs,' Ali remembered.

'But they're against the European Federation,' Luciel insisted. 'And that includes the Hex laws.'

'The fact that they've attempted to get in touch with us suggests they might support the Hex cause,' Wraith agreed. 'But we would have to be careful in contacting them and I don't know where would be a safe place to meet.'

'Isn't here safe enough?' Ali asked, alarmed. 'Finn and Jeeva said this was one of the best set-ups they'd seen.'

'In negotiations like this it's generally considered unwise to reveal the location of your home base,' Wraith explained. He didn't want to put Ali down but he was aware that despite her efforts to help the group she was still inexperienced. 'Customarily one arranges a meeting on neutral territory.'

'Then maybe we could go through the Countess,' Luciel suggested, thinking quickly. 'She passed on the message originally and her place is well defended. Perhaps we could meet Anglecynn there.'

'It's a good idea,' Wraith said approvingly. 'If the Countess will agree.'

'I'll go and ask Jeeva,' Luciel said. 'He's supposed to be heading back to her building. He can ask her if she'll be a go-between.'

'All right,' Wraith agreed. 'Once you've done that you should try and get some sleep. There's nothing more we can do today and we'll need to be alert tomorrow.'

'What about you?' Ali asked. 'You're still recovering.'

'I've already rested,' Wraith replied. 'And we'll need to take shifts in the control room, just in case the CPS or the Seccies have managed to track us here.'

'I still can't believe Cloud betrayed us,' Ali said quietly. 'He must hate Hexes.'

'A lot of people do,' Luciel said softly. 'The government tries to make us seem dangerous so no one will object to the extermination laws. No one really knows what Hexes are like.'

'It's really Avalon he betrayed,' Wraith said. 'The rest of us didn't even know him but she trusted him. That kind of betrayal is difficult to accept.'

The officials from the Security Services had left hours ago but Cloud still sat where they had interviewed him. The other members of Masque had returned that evening to find Security Services operatives searching the residence while Cloud was questioned in a private room. Once the Seccies had left they tried to find out what had happened but all Cloud had told them was that Avalon had gone. Corin and Jesse had tried to get him to tell them more but

Cloud stayed silent and Lissa's concern for the future of the band had infected them all.

'Without Avalon we're nothing,' she had exclaimed bitterly. 'What are we supposed to do without her?'

Cloud had left them arguing and returned to his room. The Security Services had asked him to turn off the holo images that normally swam through the air and without them his room was stark and empty.

Avalon had accused him of betraying her and he knew she was right. The questions the Seccies had asked him had made it clear that the strangers had not only been terrorists but Hexes as well and suddenly Avalon's final words to him had made sense. He'd meant to protect her from a foolish decision. Instead it seemed he'd endangered her life. Even if the Seccies didn't yet suspect that Avalon might be a Hex as well, they would soon. Then she'd be in greater danger than if he'd just allowed her to leave with the strangers and made up some excuse for her disappearance. Avalon's face was known across the world. There was hardly a person in the city who wouldn't recognize her and once she was known to be a Hex every hand would be turned against her.

That's my responsibility, Cloud thought to himself, staring blankly at the walls of his white room. *And there's nothing I can do.*

8
Two Chained Bullets

The call came through just after dawn. Alaric got up sleepily as his com signal chimed and answered it, yawning.

'Alaric here,' he said, rubbing the sleep from his eyes. 'What's up?'

'This is Liz,' the voice on the other end of the signal informed him. 'You have a message from a fixer called the Countess.'

'I'm on my way down,' Alaric informed her and turned the wristcom off. Jordan was still asleep, and he dressed quietly so as not to disturb her and headed down to the computer room. To his surprise Liz was waiting for him with a cup of coffee substitute and she seemed unusually communicative.

'I'm sorry to wake you,' she said. 'But everyone's stirred up since the discussion about joining with the Hexes and I thought this might be relevant.'

'I hope so,' Alaric replied, taking the cup and seating himself at one of the terminals. 'But they might not be interested in meeting with us.'

He called the message up, using his personal cipher to access the message. When it came it was terse and to the point.

'Negotiations can commence at your convenience. Location: my premises. Each group may bring four

members. Weapons to be surrendered on arrival.'

Alaric moved aside so that Liz could see the screen and she nodded approvingly.

'Good conditions,' she said. 'You going?'

'I think I should,' Alaric replied. 'Who else do you suggest?'

'Geraint,' she said instantly. 'It balances opinions since he is still uncertain.'

'And if he's uncertain he needs to see what they're like,' Alaric agreed. 'If he changes his mind most of the other dissenters will as well and if he doesn't there's probably a good reason for it.'

'What about Daniel?' Liz asked. 'He knows one of them.'

'He's still a new member,' Alaric replied. 'I'd rather take people with more experience. Maybe Jordan.'

Liz smiled and Alaric felt annoyed. Jordan was an experienced member of Anglecynn. He wouldn't have suggested her otherwise. He was surprised when Liz said thoughtfully:

'Jordan might be a good idea. She doesn't look like a terrorist.'

'And I do?'

'Don't be dense.' Liz looked irritated. 'Jordan's obviously less of a threat – she's young and female. If they're alarmed by us, she might convince them to be more forthcoming.'

'Conversely then, the fourth member of the party should be someone who does look like a terrorist,' Alaric suggested. 'Just in case they're not alarmed by us and think of trying something.'

'Good idea,' said Liz approvingly and moved away from the terminal. 'I'll leave you to organize it.'

With that she left the room and Alaric turned back to

the message, composing an equally brief reply. A meeting like this had to be arranged as quickly as possibly in case anyone else got to hear of it. The Countess's reputation was good but the longer he waited to commence negotiations the greater the chance her security might slip and compromise the meeting. Tonight, he decided, keying a reply on to the terminal. That way there'd be the cover of dark in case anything went wrong.

'2200 hours. Will comply with conditions.'

He sent the message and turned off the terminal. He'd need to discuss this with some of the other veterans before he officially decided who should go. He hoped they'd be as relieved as him that the Hex group had made contact.

Avalon was on duty in the control room. The other members of the group had taken shifts through the night and Finn and Jeeva had left saying they'd be back in the morning with the Countess's reply. Avalon had offered to take the dawn watch and was spending the time familiarizing herself with the security system. She was impressed by the effectiveness of the system Raven had designed and she wanted to understand how to use it. She suspected the group had little use for a musician and she needed something to do. She'd noticed how inexperienced the young Hexes were and how useless they'd felt while Wraith was out of action. Now they seemed to be taking more of a role in decision making and Avalon didn't want to be left behind as a worthless member of the group.

She was still trying to get to know the others but so far she'd only talked much to Finn, who wasn't really one of them. She'd found herself liking the Snake gangers for the way they'd instantly taken charge of the situation when they arrived at the base. The Hex group had obviously been thrown by the loss of Raven and Avalon suspected it was because the dark-haired girl had taken most of the decisions. From their discussion in the hotel room it seemed clear that she'd taught the others very little, if anything, of what she knew and they were handicapped without her.

Is it that she doesn't trust them, she wondered. *Or does she deliberately try to keep them dependent on her?*

They were a disparate bunch of people without very much in common. But something held them together as a group despite their seeming differences. The arrangement reminded Avalon of Masque. None of the band members, except perhaps Corin and Jesse, had very much in common. Lissa had been a child star and in the music business all her life in various different groups, never sinking very low or rising very high until she joined Masque. Corin and Jesse were both talented musicians who'd grown to be friends in the group but played very different styles of music. Avalon had worked her way from the slums to megastardom in a meteoric leap and Cloud came from the upper echelons of society, where he'd been privileged all his life.

Thinking about Cloud gave Avalon a sinking feeling. All her life she'd been careful not to trust other people too much and the one time she'd really needed to follow that rule she'd discarded it. She knew Cloud had thought that in some strange way he was helping her, but he had also unequivocally rejected the Hex group as terrorists. If he'd known she was a Hex as well he'd probably have sold her out too to save himself. Thinking about Cloud reminded Avalon that there might be media coverage of her disappearance.

Does everyone know I'm a Hex now? she wondered. *Or haven't the CPS guessed that's how I was involved?*

She fumbled with the notes she'd made about how to operate the control system, searching for the correct keypad. Eventually she found it and a large vidscreen turned on, showing a transmission from one of the entertainment feeds. She channel surfed for a while, trying to find some form of news, and stopped when she saw an image of Masque's palatial residence. There were media flitters clustered around it and a few other craft marked with the logo of the Security Services.

'. . . *still searching for the singer Avalon,*' the newscaster was saying, '. . . *who disappeared yesterday in mysterious circumstances from her home in the heights of London. The Security Services were on the scene today but declined to give any statement, although sources within the Ministry of Security have suggested that the singer's disappearance is connected to the capture of the terrorists responsible for yesterday's blackout. However, other members of Masque have strongly refuted those claims.*'

The image cut to an interview with Lissa, Corin and Jesse. They all looked worried and harassed. Avalon could imagine how the media networks must have been badgering them to give some kind of statement.

'*Avalon wouldn't have had anything to do with terrorists,*' Jesse was asserting fiercely. '*In all the time I've known her she's never done anything like that. A lot of people in this industry have tried to bend the law in one way or another but Avalon's completely honest.*'

'*I can't believe anyone would suggest that,*' Corin agreed. '*At the moment we think Avalon may have been kidnapped and if anyone has any information about her whereabouts please call our record company's hotline. We're very worried about her.*'

'*How will this affect Masque's future?*' the interviewer

asked and Avalon frowned to herself as she watched.

'Avalon is still the lead singer of Masque,' Lissa said quickly, *'and we're all anxious to have her back – but she's not the only member of the group and we're all still involved in creative projects of our own. Until Avalon returns we'll be concentrating on those for a while.'*

The vidscreen cut again back to a news anchor standing in front of Masque's residence.

'Cloud Estavisti, Masque's enigmatic dancer and holo-artist, was unavailable for comment today. Despite repeated requests from the media he has declined to give any statement. Perhaps his silence suggests another reason for Avalon's absence: could the two megastars have quarrelled? Perhaps this signals a split for Masque. We now return to the studio to discuss the implications of this breaking story.'

Avalon turned off the vidscreen decisively. She had no wish to see what conclusions the media were going to jump to. Lissa seemed to have made it clear that the band would be trying to survive without Avalon before their news value disappeared. Cloud's absence confused her. She had been expecting him to throw her to the wolves. But perhaps he was being questioned since he had called the Seccies in the first place. She found herself hoping that they made his life as difficult as possible.

Sir Charles Alverstead regarded the dancer dubiously. He had hoped that the capture of Raven would prevent any further action by the Hex terrorists but the disappearance of Avalon had gravely concerned him. He had ordered an immediate check on the megastar's medical records only to find that Avalon had never seen a doctor in her life. Her background was known to be from the slums of the city and she had missed out on the routine medical examinations normally performed on children. In the circumstances it was highly possible she was a rogue Hex and he disliked the possibility that the terrorists had lost one dangerous member only to acquire another. He had sent for Cloud Estavisti to attempt to find out more about the singer but Cloud was being uncooperative.

'This is a matter of the highest security,' he informed the dancer coldly. 'Failing to provide the Security Services with information is a crime under Federation law.'

'I've told you all I know,' Cloud replied. Despite the questioning he had kept his composure even when Alverstead had refused to allow him a lawyer present. 'I discovered a group of armed strangers entering the residence and called the Security Services immediately. By the time they arrived the strangers were gone and so was Avalon. I've given you their descriptions. There's nothing more I can tell you.'

Alverstead looked annoyed.

'I'll be honest with you, Mr Estavisti,' he said. 'More honest than I suspect you are being with me. Avalon is currently under suspicion of possessing the Hex gene and I suspect you know more than you are telling us. The Federation Council allows the CPS wide powers of jurisdiction where Hexes are concerned and if you are not more helpful I have the power to hold you here until you are.'

'I understand that, Governor,' Cloud said calmly. 'I could point out that the CPS would become the focus of a lot of media attention if you continue to hold me here. But, as it is, I shall simply say I can give you nothing more. If I could help you further I'd be glad to – this sort of speculation isn't going to do my career any good. But there's really nothing else I can tell you.'

Alverstead considered Cloud carefully. He couldn't rid

himself of the belief that the dancer knew more than he was saying but Cloud's continued calm caused him to doubt his instincts. He was also aware that the CPS depended on the media's lack of interest in their activities. If he did hold Cloud it might lead to unfortunate questions about the way the agency operated. If the general public were to find out about the experimentation Alverstead's job would become much more difficult. He decided not to risk it. Kalden had promised that there would soon be results from the experiments he was performing on Raven. In the circumstances this matter of the missing rock star couldn't be allowed to interfere.

'Very well, Mr Estavisti,' he said. 'I will release you for the time being. But make sure you are available for future questioning. I wouldn't want you to disappear as well.'

'I assure you I do not intend to,' Cloud replied, before being ushered out of Alverstead's office.

Cloud was escorted back to his luxury flitter by armed guards but he didn't lose any of his composure. His chauffeur opened the door of the flitter for him and he stretched out inside, looking through the window at the European Federation building. Armed guards surrounded it, giving an ominous appearance to the dark skyscraper section.

'Where to, sir?' the chauffeur asked politely.

'Back to the residence,' Cloud replied. 'But take a long route.' He wasn't eager to return home, what with the media watching the place like hawks and the suspicion that the Seccies and the CPS would probably be keeping an eye on him. The other members of the band were still pestering him for an explanation of Avalon's disappearance. He had told them the same story he'd told Alverstead but they didn't believe him any more than the CPS Governor had seemed to. The other members of

Masque were used to Cloud's unruffled appearance. Lissa had once asked him if anything ever surprised him. Cloud was frequently surprised but the image he projected of cool unconcern was part of his mystique. He had cultivated it, aware that people found mysteries fascinating. Now it seemed that pose of indifference had saved him from being locked in a CPS cell until he provided Alverstead with more information. Cloud was relieved but he didn't trust that the reprieve would last. Alverstead was still suspicious. Under other circumstances Cloud would have left the city, maybe even the country, until the mess could be sorted out and the media had forgotten the incident. But Alverstead had warned him not to drop out of sight.

Watching the view of the city flash past his window, Cloud considered the problem. Ideally he would like to warn Avalon of the CPS's suspicions but in the circumstances she was probably aware of her danger. Danger that he had caused. Cloud wrenched his mind away from that thought and tried to concentrate. He had warned Avalon against the terrorists honestly. Now he was caught up in the kind of mess he'd hoped he could help her avoid.

Poetic justice, he thought to himself. *But what do I do next?*

Raven had expected the experiments to begin again the next day but when the guards arrived to open the cell they came with two strangers, men in expensive dark suits who looked at the prisoners with faint disgust. Dr Kalden was with them and looked annoyed at the interruption of his experiments. Kez looked at them in alarm but Raven considered them carefully. She recognized Adam Hammond the Security Minister almost immediately.

She'd seen him on newscasts and wasn't entirely surprised to see him now. The other man took her longer to identify. The CPS tended not to issue many statements and most of its officials tended to remain anonymous. But Raven had been understandably interested in the subject and after a few moments she placed the second visitor as Sir Charles Alverstead.

'This is her then?' Alverstead asked. 'She doesn't look more than a child.'

'This is Raven,' Kalden confirmed. 'She may look young but she's one of the most interesting subjects I've ever had.'

'She's been confined here since her capture, sir,' Adam Hammond added. 'I hope the arrangements are to your satisfaction?'

'They seem to be adequate,' Alverstead agreed. 'Who's this other child?'

Kez looked with concern at Raven who silenced him with a warning look.

'Another dangerous prisoner,' she said drily. 'Who doubtless will also be executed once you've contravened European law in twenty different ways by experimenting on him as well.'

Alverstead looked at Raven in surprise.

'You're very certain of yourself, girl,' he said coldly. Raven laughed.

'Between this cage and the activities of your paid torturer, I don't have much more to fear,' she said wryly. Unlike Kez she hadn't got up when they arrived and she looked up at Alverstead sarcastically from where she sat cross-legged on the floor. 'But I'm sure I'll be a model prisoner once Dr Kalden has finished his experimentation.'

Alverstead looked shocked and Adam Hammond

looked quickly at Dr Kalden. Kalden's blue eyes narrowed angrily. But his voice was level when he spoke.

'Perhaps you'd like to look at my initial results, Governor?'

'Yes, I think so,' Sir Charles agreed, turning away from Raven. Kez said nothing as the visitors left the room and Raven also watched them leave expressionlessly. Her diversion had prevented Alverstead from enquiring too much about Kez but sooner or later Kalden would decide he was worthless as a test subject. She doubted that Kez would be released. As a streetrat there wasn't any record of his existence anyway; it wouldn't be difficult for the CPS to dispose of him quietly without anyone finding out.

Jeeva and Finn arrived at the base at mid-morning with more equipment. The group were reaching the limit of their available creds but there'd been enough left for some more basic necessities like the Nutromac unit the Snake gangers unloaded from their flitter. Luciel set it up in the apartment suite upstairs and immediately dialled a meal for everyone. They ate in the sparsely decorated dining room and Wraith began the conversation by asking Finn if the Countess had agreed to host the meeting with Anglecynn.

'She says it's chill,' Finn told him. 'They've asked to meet this evening. The Countess says you can bring four people and so can they.'

'We still don't even know what they want,' Ali said cautiously.

'Then we'll find out tonight,' Wraith replied. 'For now we need to find out more about what happened to Raven. We don't even know if she's being held in the city.'

'Most dangerous prisoners are taken to London

prison,' Finn said thoughtfully. 'But there are other jails in the city and CPS facilities as well. She could really be anywhere.'

'The newsfeeds said she would be exterminated,' Wraith said uneasily.

'The government would never waste an opportunity to study someone like Raven,' Luciel said confidently. 'Not after the effort they put into the experiments on us.'

'If the CPS are performing experiments on her she'll be at one of their facilities,' Jeeva put in.

'But not all the CPS know about the experiments,' Ali told him. 'The government tries to keep them secret.'

'Then she'll be held somewhere secret,' Avalon suggested. 'That's not going to be easy to find out.'

'I'll contact the Countess and ask her to compile a list of possibilities,' Wraith said. 'Although the fee will probably take the rest of our creds.'

'Ali and I can do it,' Luciel suggested. 'The information's probably all on the net – we don't need to be hackers to find it.'

Wraith glanced at Ali but she didn't raise any objections to being volunteered so he nodded.

'All right,' he said. 'We'd better get to work then.'

'Before you start,' Avalon interjected, 'there's something I'd like to suggest.' The others turned to look at her and she continued: 'If you . . . we are going to try and break Raven out of wherever she's being held, Ali and Luciel will need some more weapons training and so will I.'

'She's right there,' Finn agreed. 'I've seen Wraith in action and Raven's a dead shot. But these kids can probably use work and I doubt you're much of a sharpshooter.'

'I can get by,' Avalon said seriously. 'But I'd like a little more experience before I get involved in an assault on a maximum security prison.'

'Jeeva and I can help you out there,' Finn told her. 'How about Ali and Luciel start work on the net while we show you some of the tricks of the trade. Once I see how you shape up we'll start work with the other two.'

'I'll monitor the control room,' Wraith offered. 'It's about time I had a look at what kind of system my sister's set up for us.'

The tests didn't begin again until the afternoon. The guards had brought them a plain meal at midday but neither Raven or Kez felt much like eating. It wasn't long after that they came to collect Raven for more experiments. She didn't object as they escorted her out of the cell and to Kalden's makeshift lab. The equipment was different today although they strapped her down to the same bed. Even before the machinery was turned on Raven was reaching out with her Hex senses. The testing was less painful than before. The scientists inserted thin needles into Raven's skin and fed data through them, using a bizarre helmet filled with more needle-like spikes to measure activity in her brain. The needles kept giving Raven electric shocks but, compared to yesterday, that wasn't anything she couldn't handle.

As the needles probed her she felt for the tug of the power cabling and found it, letting its flow soothe her as she was carried towards a connection to the net. It was far away and faint. If it wasn't for the needles connecting her to an electric current Raven doubted she would have found it at all. Her phantom presence slipped through the data streams of the net, observing them but unable to affect them.

Observe then, Raven told herself firmly and fell further

into the net. She passed through unknown systems like a ghost, leaving nothing behind. Through routes she'd travelled thousands of times before, made suddenly unfamiliar by her strange fragile connection to the net, she made her way back to her old computer terminal. The sleeper programmes she'd left in place were still running although there'd been some clumsy attempt to break her security precautions. In contrast Revenge's terminal was a riddled corpse. The CPS operatives had been through the girl's programming like locusts and there was little left to suggest what Revenge had done to cause the blackout. Raven left it and moved on, drifting towards the edge of the net, the part that belonged to the gangland systems. Everything was darker here and bulletin board systems issued warnings of the increase in Seccie activity.

Not my problem right now, Raven thought and slid onwards though the data paths. She was looking for the Countess's system but as she moved slowly towards it her attention was arrested by something unusual.

To Raven's Hex perceptions most of the systems which interfaced with the net were crude and ugly. Only a few had any trace of elegance or subtlety. But as she drifted across the network her attention had been caught by one spider-silk filament, tenuously connecting a computer system to the net. She reached for the silk only to feel it slip away. But now she was certain. She had spun this web herself. It was with a sense of coming home that she relaxed into it and followed its path to a system she had designed. There was no security at all, no ice to keep intruders out. But the system was hard to find, the delicacy of its pathways making it almost invisible in the crowded world of the net.

Raven floated inside the system, watching it. Only one

terminal was in use, one connecting the system to the network, and someone was scanning slowly, painstakingly slowly, through the net's public databases.

Looking for prisons, she thought with some amusement. *I could save you the trouble if I wasn't so far away.*

But distance didn't have to matter. She'd studied the Hex abilities more thoroughly than Kalden ever had and she'd yet to find any proof that distance limited them. It was the test equipment that was blocking her, filling her brain with extraneous signals that she had to ignore even as it gave her access to the electronic universe. Deliberately Raven removed her own blocks, allowing herself consciousness of all those random signals of gibberish being fed into her body. Pain stabbed at her like hundreds of tiny knives. She didn't ignore it. She just refused to allow it to interfere with what she was doing. Then, carefully, she reached out and *touched* the system.

She could imagine the panic of the user as the system suddenly froze, the keypad no longer inputting search parameters into the terminal. Meticulously careful, she sent the message she wanted to the screen.

> identify yourself <

There was a pause while Raven freed the system again and watched. The other user did nothing and she called upon her patience to send again:

> this is RAVEN – identify yourself < She was almost certain that the unknown user was a member of their group but if not, no one from the CPS would believe she was Raven if they knew her to be in custody.

> this is Ali and Luciel < the reply came haltingly, tapped slowly onto the keypad. **> Raven, is that really you? <**

If she'd been there in reality Raven would have shaken

her head at the sheer stupidity of that question. Instead she sent them the information they needed.

> with Kez in EF Consulate. will make escape attempt shortly. give details of your situation <

> you must prove your ID first. you could be CPS <

Rage flooded Raven at the answer even though intellectually she could approve of their caution. But the anger threatened to tear her away from the link with the net and she controlled herself. Reaching for the system with all the energy left to her she caused her image to appear on the terminal screen. Black hair in elf locks, black eyes shadowed with exhaustion, dead white skin. No hacker or CPS operative could have done this. The image she spun could only be caused by a Hex. She made the lips of the image move then blanked the screen and sent her message once more with the last of her strength.

> I am RAVEN <

Then the system, the shining lines of the net, the world of the Hex, shattered and collapsed into darkness as pain exploded in her head and Raven mercifully blacked out.

Ali and Luciel looked at each other. Then Luciel tentatively touched the keypad, tapping out an enquiry. There was no response and he sat back in his seat.

'She's gone,' he said. 'I wish I'd asked if she was all right.'

'She probably wouldn't have appreciated it,' said Ali numbly.

They looked at each other for a long moment. Neither of them had the skill or the experience to do what Raven had done, spinning the strands of the web from confinement to reach them, but in receiving her message they had had their first glimpse of what the other Hex experienced. The terminal had become a gateway, stretching into uncharted territory, and across that unimaginable distance Raven had reached out and touched them.

'At least she's well enough to use the net,' Luciel said finally. 'I wonder how she got to a terminal.'

'Maybe she didn't.' Ali stood up. 'Raven wouldn't let that stop her. Come on, we'd better go and find Wraith. This is something he needs to know.'

'You're right,' Luciel agreed. 'And our search is over anyway. Raven's given us the information we needed.'

9

Lightning Moves Slow

Everyone was on edge when they set off for the Countess's building. Ali and Luciel had recounted their visitation from Raven and everyone was feeling somewhat stunned by it. Wraith was relieved just to know she was alive but he worried that they hadn't been able to make any real arrangements for her escape. Luciel was concerned that Kalden might have experimented on her and Ali was simply awestruck by the extent of Raven's abilities. Only Raven could have contacted them from a maximum security facility and she doubted that she would ever be able to use her Hex abilities that well herself. Avalon was uneasy about being recognized. She wore a woollen cap to disguise her red hair and a long army coat Jeeva had lent her.

Jeeva and Finn piloted the flitter that took them to the Countess's centre of operations. There were two armed guards on the bridge across to her section of skyscraper and they watched expressionlessly as the group got out of the flitter. Wraith took the lead with Finn; Ali and Luciel followed, both armed with the laser pistols they'd been practising with; Avalon and Jeeva brought up the rear. The guards on the bridge stopped them but only for a cursory word; everyone except Avalon was already known to them. There were more guards inside the building, some barring the route up, others scattered around the main foyer. Three of them were Snakes, with the same dyed-blue hair as Finn and Jeeva, and the two gangers melted away from the party to join them. The others removed their weapons and allowed the Countess's people to search them. Then they were led up the mirror-shielded staircase to the Countess's main room. She was waiting for them, in the middle of the customary litter of electrical components, her body covered with remote controls and mini-terminal units.

'Come in,' she told them, as the mirrored panel began to slide shut. 'Your contacts haven't arrived yet but that's as it should be.' She gestured to them to sit down at an oval table in the corner of the room, around which eight chairs had been placed. 'Once Anglecynn are here I'll leave you to biz,' she said. 'But while you're waiting you can tell me how the new place is working out.'

'It's going well,' Wraith assured her. 'The building is perfect for our needs and the security system Raven designed was set up by your technicians yesterday. We're very grateful for your assistance.'

'Nonsense.' The Countess's eyes gleamed brightly. 'Raven paid me in advance for setting you up. If I didn't fulfil my contracts what would happen to my rep?' Her eyes flitted across them and came to rest on Avalon. 'You've got a famous face,' she remarked, 'for all that you're dressed like Raven. Are you intending to replace her?'

'From what I've seen and heard so far, I think Raven's almost certainly irreplaceable,' Avalon replied. 'But I suppose I'm standing in for her.'

The Countess nodded quickly, her movements quick and birdlike.

'That's true enough,' she said. 'And since you're with friends I'll tell you something for nothing. The Seccies are on your case. They've been looking for you since yesterday afternoon and word on the streets is they're freakin' serious about it. I'd stay disguised if I was you.'

'I intend to,' Avalon assured her but she looked alarmed and Ali smiled at her reassuringly.

'They've been looking for us for a year,' she told Avalon. 'And, if it wasn't for Revenge – and she couldn't help herself – they wouldn't have found us yet.'

'And Cloud,' Avalon reminded her. 'He's to blame as well for this mess. If it hadn't been for him no one would even know I'd left.'

'There's no point dissecting it now,' Wraith interrupted and the Countess agreed.

'No point at all,' she said. 'Especially since your contacts seem to have arrived.'

The others clustered around her to watch the vidscreen image of the foyer. A sleek customized flitter had arrived and people were getting out of it. The first to emerge was a large muscular man, his arms tattooed with a pattern of entwined dragons.

'Stupid,' the Countess snorted. 'Why not just write the word "terrorist" on your head if you want to be noticed?'

She fell silent as the rest of the Anglecynn members got out, four in total. There were two more men, both quite young and not as burly as the first, and a teenage girl carrying a gun that looked incongruous against her slight frame. The guards stepped forward and all four surrendered their weapons and allowed themselves to be searched. Then the guards waved them onwards and the small party began to move towards the staircase. The Countess touched a keypad and the image disappeared. She checked over the various controls she wore as armbands and then bobbed her head at Wraith.

'They're clean,' she said and as she spoke she touched a

control and the door to the stairway slid open. The Anglecynn members were revealed on the other side and the Countess waved them in. 'Come in,' she told them. 'No need to block the door. Since you're all wanted criminals let's not waste time with formalities. You can introduce yourselves.' She turned to Wraith. 'You've got one hour, so make your conversation count. I'll be back then.'

With that she turned and left the room by another door which opened as she approached it and slid shut behind her.

Wraith watched her leave then he faced the newcomers. Extending his hand, he introduced himself.

'I'm Wraith, and this is Ali, Luciel and Avalon.'

One of the Anglecynn members reached to take his hand and shook it.

'Alaric,' he said politely. 'This is Geraint, Bryson and Jordan.'

There was a pause as all eight of them assembled around the Countess's oval table, then Alaric opened the negotiations.

'I was hoping to meet Raven,' he began. 'I was sorry to hear of her capture. She had the Seccies on the run for a long time.'

'That hasn't changed,' Wraith replied. 'Despite what you may have heard, Raven is still alive.'

'I'm pleased to hear it,' Alaric replied. 'Especially since it was largely because of Raven that I decided to contact you.'

'It was?' Wraith asked with polite curiosity and Alaric nodded agreement.

'My group is often interested in forming new contacts,' he explained. 'But what led us to meet with you is information we received from one of our agents. He came into possession of details of the latest Security Service orders. We'd expected there to be increased attempts to eradicate Anglecynn because of our recent protests but as it happened your group proved to be the focus of their latest campaign. When I checked out your details I was sure there was more to your story than the official government version.' He looked straight at Ali and smiled. 'And if you are Alison Tarrell, I believe my suspicions have been proved true.'

'How do you know about Ali?' Luciel said protectively. 'What's she got to do with this?'

'My information made reference to "missing test subjects" and Alison Tarrell's name was one of them, as was the name Luciel Liechtmann,' Alaric explained. 'A member of Anglecynn identified Alison Tarrell as being the name of a teenager who was taken by the CPS last year for possessing the Hex gene and officially registered as legally exterminated. Since no one who was exterminated could be considered missing and nothing I know about the CPS says they can use Hexes as test subjects, I reached the conclusion that there was more to your group than is commonly known. That led me to think that the lab you blew up last year wasn't a regular CPS facility at all.'

'All that may be true,' Wraith replied. 'But what has it got to do with you?'

'Anglecynn is dedicated to fighting EF control,' Alaric told him. 'That includes the Hex laws. I was hoping we might pool some of our knowledge and maybe resources as well.'

'We'd like to know something more about you first, though,' the man named Geraint added. 'The prejudice against Hexes may have been propagated by the government but even so none of us know anything about you, or what you can do.'

'That seems to be a common problem,' Luciel whispered to Ali and she giggled. Wraith turned and glared at them.

'We don't know much about you either,' he replied. 'Perhaps we could share the history of how our respective groups were formed?'

'Sounds good to me,' Bryson said cheerfully and Jordan smiled glowingly.

Wraith began the account with the same story he had told Avalon. Although it was only a day ago, it already seemed like for ever. The Anglecynn members all listened intently; Alaric in particular seemed surprised at Wraith's admission that he was not a Hex. Ali, Luciel and Avalon all appended their own stories and Wraith ended the account with the blackout, Revenge's death and Raven and Kez's capture. When he finished no one spoke for a while.

'Our story seems mundane in comparison,' Geraint said finally. 'We haven't had quite so rough a ride as you.'

'Geraint and I founded Anglecynn three years ago,' Alaric explained. 'We were still in college and studying politics. We got to reading Federation law and decided we didn't like the sound of it. So we ran a couple of student protests against EF control. We didn't take it very seriously back then but the government obviously did.'

'We were sent down from university and were put on Seccie files as political agitators. After that we decided that was exactly what we wanted to be. Alaric came up with the idea of Anglecynn and we started recruiting. We've been involved in a lot of demonstrations and a few more forceful protests but we generally try not to hurt people unless it's absolutely necessary.'

'At the moment there are about sixty of us,' Alaric explained. 'Although that includes the administrative staff who support our cause but don't get involved in protests. We've got plenty of firepower but we're lacking information and, from the sound of it, that's what your group can provide.'

'Under normal circumstances,' Wraith agreed. 'Although at the moment we're lacking Raven which curtails our sphere of influence considerably.'

'So how would you feel about an agreement of mutual assistance?' Geraint asked. 'Seeing as we have a common enemy.'

'That would depend on how your people feel about Hexes,' Wraith replied and Geraint looked uneasy.

'I admit to having qualms myself,' he said. 'But so far what you've said seems to check out. Most of Anglecynn seem keen on the idea.'

'That's true,' Jordan agreed. 'And apart from us, you've done the most harm to the Federation. A lot of our people admire you for that. And we're always sympathetic to people who've been persecuted.'

Dr Kalden hissed with irritation. Another routine experiment with equipment that had been tested extensively and now the subject had lost consciousness. One of his team hurriedly checked Raven over while the others rechecked the equipment.

'I think she fainted,' the scientist said after a while. 'It must have been the electric current. Maybe she's not in as good a condition as some of our earlier subjects or maybe she's just unusually sensitive to the test equipment.'

'Interesting,' Kalden mused, losing his flinty expression. 'If it's a matter of sensitivity this could represent a breakthrough for us. But we can't continue the testing if she's going to pass out like this all the time. We obviously need another approach.'

He looked at the slim black-clad figure lying on the bed and wondered what secrets the mutant's mind held. She was indubitably his greatest challenge, he thought. If only she could understand the importance of science she would be proud to sacrifice herself to his experiments.

'But they never do understand,' he mused out loud and noticed the other scientists looking at him oddly. 'Take her back to her cell,' he ordered. 'I need time to consider a new approach.'

When the hour the Countess had stipulated was up the two groups parted and agreed to meet again in the future. Alaric had things to discuss with the rest of Anglecynn and the Hex group needed to make plans to rescue Raven. However both sides felt that the meeting had gone well. The last thing Alaric said before his party left was that he would try to persuade Anglecynn to make the Hex right to life a central point of their constitution.

'After that, if there's one thing we've experience with it's media manipulation,' Alaric said. 'People deserve to know the truth about the way the Hexes are treated.'

Once the flitter had left the Countess's building and was sailing back to the depths of the city, Alaric noticed Geraint was silent and thoughtful.

'What did you think of them?' he asked quietly and the other veteran shrugged.

'They seemed honest, and those Hex kids they have certainly aren't any kind of threat.'

'But . . . ?' Alaric prompted.

'It's Raven I'm wondering about,' Geraint admitted. 'From the sound of it, she worked out that lab existed then planned a military assault on it. But she didn't think of a way to rescue the other children in the experiments. From the way they talk it sounds like all of them are in awe of her, except maybe Wraith. That worries me.'

'I thought Raven sounded wonderful,' Jordan said quietly. 'The anti-EF front needs heroes and she's the kind of person we could admire. I always thought no Hexes ever escaped extermination. But Raven saved three or four people from it and risked her life over and over again to do it. That's real heroism. It just makes it better that she's not much more than a child herself.'

'It didn't sound much like heroism to me,' Geraint objected but Bryson interrupted him.

'I like the idea of us having a hero, some kind of symbol for the cause. Sounds to me like this Raven would be a good candidate.'

'Even though she's a Hex,' Alaric asked curiously.

'That's good too,' Jordan said enthusiastically. 'Knowing that someone you thought was normal is a Hex is a shock for people. But heroes are supposed to be extraordinary and have special powers. People won't mind that Raven's a Hex, they might even start thinking about Hexes differently when they hear about her.'

Daniel had been thinking about going to sleep when Alaric arrived back at Dragon's Nest and sent out the call for a general meeting. Instead he staked out a place in the common room and waited for everyone to arrive. As the room filled rumours began to circulate about the purpose of this meeting.

'Alaric went to meet the Hexes,' he heard a girl called Maggie saying. 'Maybe he's brought one of them back with him.'

'Not without consulting everyone,' someone else contradicted. 'But I bet this is to tell us about them.'

Daniel wondered whether Ali Tarrell had been one of the Hexes Alaric had met. He found it hard to imagine one of his sister's socialite friends as a member of a dangerous terrorist group. But then he found it hard to imagine himself as one either. Yet here he was, part of Anglecynn's private councils, living in a deserted slum building in the city's cavernous roots. His mind drifted as he wondered what Caitlin and his father were doing now. Caitlin was probably watching a mindless holovid programme, while his father worked late at the Ministry. He was surprised not to feel any nostalgia for his past life; already it seemed years ago.

He snapped back to reality as Alaric came into the room. Geraint, Jordan and Bryson arrived at the same time and all four of them found seats near the centre of the room, other people moving up to give them more space.

'I'm sorry to have to call a meeting so late,' Alaric began. 'But I know a lot of you have been anxious to know the results of the negotiations with the Hexes and we have a lot of new information you should hear about.' He gestured at the three people sitting close to him. 'All four of us went to the meeting so all I'm going to give you now is a summary of what happened. Then we can split for discussion and we'll tell you more about what their group was like. After that there are some questions I'd like to take to a vote.'

'Get on with it then!' someone called from the back and everyone laughed. Alaric smiled in return and began his account.

The members of Anglecynn were used to stories of atrocities. That was one of the reasons they'd chosen to fight the European Federation. But they were shocked when Alaric told them the story of the CPS lab the Hexes had attacked and the experiments performed on children. Daniel felt sickened by the tale. What had shocked him the most was that until recently he hadn't even thought about the plight of the Hexes. But for years they had been murdered, tortured and shunned without anyone lifting a hand to stop it. Across the room there were murmurs of disgust, echoing his own feelings. None of them questioned the truth of the tale. Some of them remembered the pictures of the test subjects that had been broadcast across the media before the government news blackout. At the time it had seemed like just another scandal. Now Alaric depicted it as a crime of epic proportions.

'I feel personally guilty for not thinking about this before,' Alaric admitted. 'I tried to get in touch with the Hexes because I thought they could be useful to us. I still think that but now I'm certain we owe them our help as well. We're supposed to be fighting EF injustice but we didn't even notice this.'

The mood of the meeting was subdued when Alaric finished his account and it took a while for the usual smaller discussions to begin. When they did, Daniel took advantage of the opportunity to ask Alaric about Ali.

'Yes, she was there,' the veteran said. 'She didn't say much apart from her part in the plan to infiltrate the laboratory. They all looked tired. I think being without Raven's been hard on them all.'

'I was just thinking I can't imagine Ali Tarrell as a terrorist but then I realized I can't think of myself as one either,' Daniel admitted.

'Good.' Alaric smiled at him. 'I don't want people here to think of themselves as terrorists. Terrorists are people who deliberately spread fear. We're fighting for a cause we believe in. We try to spread enlightenment and the people who are afraid of that are the ones who call us terrorists.'

Daniel nodded and then asked, 'What proposals are you going to put to a vote?'

'I think we should try and finish what the Hexes started,' Alaric explained. 'Release the records of what the CPS has been doing to the media, start getting people to think about the fact that under EF law Hexes have no rights and that most Hexes the CPS catch are children who don't even know what crime they're punished for.'

'The Seccies won't like that,' Daniel warned.

'Since when did the Seccies like anything about us?' Alaric responded and Daniel had to admit that he was right.

After a while the room calmed down enough for Alaric to put forward his proposals. Most people agreed instantly. Quite apart from the justice of the cause most of them were tired of being cooped up in Dragon's Nest and were eager to start a new campaign. But there were a few dissenters as usual.

'It's madness to get involved with this just when the Seccies aren't interested in us,' one of them pointed out. 'Right now they couldn't care less about Anglecynn, they're all too busy helping the CPS catch Hexes. But if we start getting involved they'll be all over us like falling garbage. We'll never get rid of them then.'

A few other people agreed but the vast majority of members were overwhelmingly in favour of a new campaign on behalf of the Hexes. The final vote came out as fifty-three to seven with four abstentions. Only then did Alaric finally call a halt to the meeting and people departed for bed.

Alaric contacted Wraith first thing the next day on a coded frequency to tell him about Anglecynn's decision and to ask for any more information about the CPS's treatment of Hexes. They had exchanged com signals so as not to have to go through the Countess every time. Wraith agreed to send all the information they had and in return Alaric promised to try to get Anglecynn help with rescuing Raven.

'I haven't put it to them yet,' he explained. 'But I'm certain they'll go for it. The way Jordan was talking the other day it sounds as if she thinks Raven qualifies for sainthood and the administrative staff are already talking about the good a known hero would do for our movement.'

'We'd be grateful for any help you could give us,' Wraith said honestly. 'We're under strength at the moment and breaking into the EF Consulate is a major operation.'

'Agreed, but we might have some info that can swing the balance,' Alaric told him. 'One of our members is Daniel Hammond, the son of the Security Minister. He's been to the Consulate and part of the information he gave us included rough maps of the building. That might just give you the edge you need, with or without Anglecynn.'

Wraith's private thought was that 'with Anglecynn' seemed the better option. He'd been impressed by what he'd seen and heard of the group and he remembered that Raven, while dismissive, had not been entirely contemptuous of their operation. Personally he preferred the idea of going on as part of an established well-trained group who were used to working together. It had been a long time since he'd missed his days in the Kali; the gangs had held too many bitter memories. But Finn's words to Avalon about trust the previous day had connected with him. He had trusted Ali and Luciel and even Avalon, although he barely knew her. But he knew they were all inexperienced and he missed the sensation of knowing someone competent was guarding his back.

When he told the rest of them about Anglecynn's plans they were enthusiastic. Luciel went off on his own to record a vid-tape account of his experiences in the lab so he could send it to Anglecynn.

'You could do something like that, as well,' Ali suggested to Avalon. 'Lots of people admire you – maybe they'd listen if you told them you're a Hex too.'

'I'll think about it,' Avalon replied. 'But I don't know if I can. I'm not sure if people are interested in what megastars have to say. Mostly they just want holosheets to stick on their walls.'

Ali didn't allow Avalon's cautious reply to spoil her good mood. She'd been cheerful ever since hearing that Daniel Hammond was a member of Anglecynn. She didn't remember him much; he'd been Caitlin's bookish older brother when she'd known him before. But the idea that Caitlin's father had announced a campaign against Hexes had hit her hard and knowing about Daniel's defection made her feel better about her involvement with the group. He seemed like a link to her old life and she hoped she'd have a chance to see him before too long and reminisce about the Belgravia Complex. It didn't occur to her to think that Daniel had left the Complex voluntarily, whereas she'd been forced to leave by the CPS discovering what she was.

Anglecynn worked fast. The media blitz began that day and the protesters took their flitters up into the city to begin the campaign at the EF Consulate. Armed with banners marked *Stop the Torture* and holo projectors with images of the child test subjects, they began their protest with a bang. The media turned up in under ten minutes and the Seccies seconds later. While the Anglecynn members bombarded the building with pictures and fact sheets, which soon started to litter the ground and blow through the city, the Seccies desperately tried to get them off the premises.

Inside the Consulate Raven and Kez were unaware of the commotion. Raven had been sleeping ever since the guards had brought her back to the cell, and Kez stayed awake to watch over her. He knew the experiments were hitting Raven badly, even though she still seemed confident that they would escape. Kez had seen what had happened to the kids in the laboratory and he wondered what Kalden was doing to Raven to leave her so weak and drained all the time. Raven had said that Kalden was doomed and Kez was beginning to dream of killing him himself. Raven and Wraith were the two people he cared about most in the world; Kalden had almost destroyed Wraith by torturing Rachel and now he was torturing Raven too. In the small cell Kez silently vowed revenge, just as Rachel must have done before him. If Raven didn't find a way to kill Kalden, he would.

10
Heaven Doth Revenge

Raven woke knowing today was the day she would have to escape. The experimentation was taking a heavy toll on her. She hadn't anticipated that she would find using her Hex abilities so painful during the experiments. Now she realized that if it continued any longer she wouldn't have the strength for an escape attempt. She would have to do it today or not at all.

With her eyes still shut she stretched herself out on the floor of the cell and concentrated. That whisper of the net she'd caught before would still be far away. But now she had found it twice during the experimentation. She hoped, that with nothing to distract her mind, her abilities would be stronger now. She reached out as far as she could and felt a single thread of the net slip by. That was enough. Wordlessly she sent her message, directing it to follow the path she couldn't take, all the way back to Wraith. Then the thread slipped away from her and she let go. There was nothing more she could do. From here on she had to conserve her energy for the escape attempt.

Across the room Kez didn't even realize that Raven was awake. He was making plans and discarding them as he had been all night. There was no way he could overpower the guards and no way out of the cell without it. He knew as well as Raven that they would have to escape soon. But he could see no way to accomplish it.

*

Outside the Consulate the Anglecynn protesters had allowed the Seccies to drive them off for a while and moved on to the New Houses of Parliament. The media went with them. Most of them were just interested in the spectacle but a couple of the channels were beginning to investigate what Anglecynn was protesting about. A few smaller pressure groups who had seen the newsfeeds joined Anglecynn at the Houses of Parliament and some of the regular people listened to what they were saying and joined in as well. It wasn't exactly a spontaneous outpouring of sympathy for the Hexes but the size of the demonstration made it difficult for the Seccies to break it up.

Avalon watched the protest on the newsfeeds. Her disappearance was still the main story on most of them. One of the channels was speculating that the reason for all the Seccie interest in Cloud was that they suspected him of Avalon's murder. Avalon felt awkward about that. Although Cloud had betrayed her she was annoyed at the media making up such a complete fantasy. She doubted any of them actually suspected Cloud was capable of murder. But now the story would spread and might harm his career.

Her musings were interrupted by a chime from the com system. She wondered vaguely about it as she touched the keypad to bring up the message then felt her body stiffen as she read it.

> come today. as soon as you can <

It had to be from Raven – no one else would have sent it – and its brevity worried Avalon. If Raven hadn't had time to send more than this it must be urgent. Accordingly she headed down the corridor to the apartment suite. She was certain to find the others there and they'd need to know about the message as soon as possible. She found Wraith first, also watching the news channels on a battered old vidcom he'd salvaged from the litter in the building. He looked up as she entered and immediately spoke:

'Avalon, what's wrong? You look concerned.'

'We've just had a message from Raven,' she explained. 'She wants us to come now, today, as soon as we can, she said.'

Wraith looked worried.

'We're not exactly ready to move yet,' he said. 'What can we do with only four people?'

'You said Anglecynn would help us,' Avalon said quickly. 'They're already causing a huge diversion. Let's get them back to the EF Consulate and mount the rescue attempt during the protest.'

'We'll have to,' Wraith replied. 'I can't think of anything else to do.'

Alaric had just been relieved from duty when the call came in. He'd been part of the demonstration at the EF building and the Houses of Parliament and had come back to Dragon's Nest for a break. But he'd only just got there when the administrative staff summoned him to answer Wraith's call. He'd not been expecting it and he hadn't had time to sound Anglecynn out about rescuing Raven but the other veterans there were willing to try. He told Wraith he'd be at the Consulate building in an hour with as much firepower as he could provide and then closed the channel. Apart from the admin people there were only twelve people in the building and he asked them to assemble in the common room.

'I wasn't expecting this to happen so soon,' he told them. 'But I've had word from the Hex group that Raven is being held in the EF Consulate and she's managed to get a message out saying she can't hold out much longer. Wraith has asked for our help and I think we should give it to him. However there isn't enough time to call a general meeting.'

'Just do it then,' Bryson encouraged him. 'We shouldn't waste our time having meetings when someone needs help – and everyone voted to help the Hexes last night anyway.'

'Not everyone,' Liz put in. 'But it makes sense to go. There won't be any objections.'

'In that case this is what I suggest,' Alaric said with some relief. 'We send the protesters back to the EF building but this time with some of the crowd-control weapons. We keep everything as confusing and troubled as we can and provide cover for a small group who'll attempt to enter the building from one of the service entrances.'

'How small?' Bryson asked. 'The place seemed quite well defended to me.'

'No more than twenty,' Alaric said. 'We'll want to move swiftly while we're inside and that means not too many people.'

'Twenty sounds good to me,' Geraint agreed. 'We'll take enough weapons for twenty people and Liz can put out a call for volunteers on the com frequencies.'

'Let's get going, then,' Alaric announced and the group scattered to get ready.

Alaric went to arrange weapons. Most of the time Anglecynn members only carried light arms but this mission would require something heavier. After considering for a while he decided on standard military blasters. They weren't the most advanced weaponry he had but all the troops had trained extensively on them and Alaric decided familiarity was the most important issue. He uncrated twenty blasters and checked each of them over carefully; then added another five in case of accidents and collected some crowd-control weaponry. Other Anglecynn members helped him load two flitters with the weapons and Liz met them in the flitter bay.

'I've got you your volunteers,' she told him. 'They'll be waiting two blocks away from the Consulate with the current protest coordinator. I've also sent word to the Hex group that's where to find you.'

'Thank you,' Alaric replied. 'Sure you don't want to come with us?'

'I prefer my excitement less lethal,' Liz replied and headed back to her work.

Meanwhile work had continued loading the flitters and Alaric took advantage of the opportunity to check over his people. They'd all found light body armour from the group's somewhat motley collection and loaded more into the flitter for the volunteers. Alaric questioned them quickly on the use of the blasters and looked over everyone for any sign that they'd be a danger to themselves or their team-mates. Once everyone checked out they got into the flitters and headed out from the Nest.

It had been over a year since Anglecynn had mounted a military-style attack. But the troops were excited as they set off and Alaric realized that someone had been spreading stories about Raven. If the team members didn't precisely consider her a hero they were certainly proud to be rescuing her and curious about meeting the other Hexes. As the flitters climbed through the city he tried to keep his part of the team in a good mood. It was important to be calm when you went into battle and not over-excited. He concentrated on projecting confidence, knowing that people relied on him to be strong, but he wasn't as calm as he looked. He remembered what Geraint had said about Raven and wondered if the other veteran was right. Raven was too much of an unknown quality for him to be entirely complacent about meeting her. But he had to help save her. If he didn't he was betraying what Anglecynn stood for and without their principles they really would deserve the name of terrorists.

Jeeva had been giving Ali a lesson with the laser pistol when Wraith came to tell her that they were moving to rescue Raven. He didn't say much and politely excused himself as Wraith began the preparations for departure. Wraith tried not to be disappointed and concentrated on making sure that Avalon, Ali and Luciel were capable of defending themselves. He'd satisfied himself that they'd at least be shooting in roughly the right direction and was about to get into the flitter when Jeeva returned, with Finn close behind him.

'Heard you're having some trouble,' Finn said. 'You going to break Raven out?'

'That's right,' Wraith told him. 'Want to come along?'

'Only if you don't,' Finn replied and the others looked at him in surprise.

'What do you mean?' Wraith asked defensively, even though he had a good idea what the ganger was talking about.

'You're not qualified to go,' Finn told him. 'If you were one of my brothers I'd order you to stay behind. You're injured, you can't shoot anything and you'll be a liability to your people. Since I can't order you to stay behind I'm asking you. If you wait here Jeeva and I will go with your people. That's two men who can shoot to replace one who can't.'

'And if I go?' Wraith asked challengingly.

'Then we don't,' Finn told him. 'But I reckon you're smarter than that, brother.'

Wraith considered for a moment then he sighed.

'All right, you win,' he said. 'I probably wouldn't be much use anyway.'

'You're right about that,' Finn agreed, taking Wraith's place in the flitter as Jeeva got in the back. 'Catch you later. We'll bring them back safely.'

Wraith didn't doubt that. But as he watched the small group depart he was conscious of feeling guilty that he wasn't with them. He controlled himself. Finn's decision had been the right one and Wraith should have made it himself. The Snake ganger had made things easier for him, knowing Wraith's judgement was suspect where Raven was concerned. Wraith was surprised how much he had come to trust the gangers but they had proved themselves dependable over recent days and Raven had considered them trustworthy as well. As he made his way back to the control room he tried to have confidence in his team, even though he wasn't part of it.

As the little flitter left Avalon looked back at the dark hulk of the building, wondering how Wraith was reacting to being so suddenly deposed.

'That was a generous thing to do,' she said to Finn.

'Wraith's a brother even though he doesn't admit it,' Finn replied. 'We've been in action together. By my code that means we owe each other. No one lets a brother go into a fight he can't possibly win.'

'That puts you in command,' Luciel told Ali and her eyes widened.

'No it doesn't!' she objected. 'Finn knows more about this sort of thing.'

'But I'm not part of your group,' Finn told her. 'There

needs to be a chain of command. If you've got seniority, you're in charge.'

'But what do I do?' Ali demanded. 'I don't know anything about strategy. The last time you did this I was the one being rescued.'

'Ask for advice when you need it and ignore it if you don't,' Jeeva told her. 'You'll get used to it.'

Ali subsided. She wasn't confident that she'd be able to see this through but she didn't want to let Luciel down and she supposed she could ask Finn for advice most of the time. She suspected there would probably be a bit more to this mission than just ordering everyone to find Raven and then ordering them out again. She concentrated on checking her gun over for the fifth time. At least that was one thing she could probably do. She might not be a great shot but she was much better than she had been. Luciel touched her arm reassuringly.

'You'll be fine,' he told her. 'You've been doing OK so far.'

'Well, just remember if I get it wrong the job's yours,' Ali told him.

Sir Charles Alverstead looked out of one of the Consulate windows at the rabble assembled below. Earlier it had looked as if they were departing. But now they were back in full force, chanting and yelling and generally causing trouble. He wasn't worried about the demonstration. The EF Consulate guards had been instructed to leave the problem to the Security Services and so far they weren't having any real problems with the protesters. He supposed this was some attempt on the part of the Hex rebels to strike back after Raven's capture. He was relieved that their reaction was something as negligible as a protest. All the same the publicity was irritating. It was fortunate that most of the protesters were from known terrorist groups. That would discredit their testimony considerably.

He was more concerned about the fact that Kalden still hadn't got any useful results from Raven. He had reported that she was showing an unusual sensitivity to the equipment, which would have to be recalibrated before further tests. But sensitivity wasn't what Alverstead was interested in. Kalden had been running his experiments for years and he was still apparently no nearer to providing any useful results. Alverstead had considered replacing him when the main testing laboratory had been destroyed but had decided against it. Kalden's lab had been the only one performing experiments and had been sited in Britain because the country was considered an insignificant power within the might of the EF. That meant that Kalden was the most experienced of all the scientists who had worked on the problem. But Alverstead had been irritated by Raven's antagonistic attitude. Usually Kalden's subjects were overcome by fear of him. Raven's attitude appeared to be contempt. He hoped he hadn't made a mistake in leaving Kalden in control of the project.

A roar from the demonstrators drew his attention back to the crowd below and he was alarmed to see a thick blue smoke rolling towards the building. Most of the protesters had retreated to the safety of their flitters although some could be seen amidst the smoke, wearing masks to protect themselves from its effects. The Seccies had no such protection and uniformed officers were staggering out of the blue clouds, bent over with fits of choking. Alverstead looked for the EF guards and saw them retreating back to the building. Crossing quickly to the vidcom unit he called their commander.

'Why are your men pulling back?' he demanded.

'We thought it was advisable—' the Commander of the Guard began, but Alverstead interrupted him.

'Have you had any orders from the Consul?'

'No, sir.'

'In that case get out there and find out what's going on. You must have gas masks, man. Use them!'

'Yes, sir!' The Commander said sharply and signed off.

Alverstead returned to the window and looked out at the crowds again. Almost all his field of vision was obscured by the blue clouds of smoke and he tapped his fingers against the window in irritation.

Raven had no way of knowing if her message had got through but when the guards arrived to collect her for the next set of tests she noticed they looked on edge. Something was obviously going on, even though she had no idea what. When she arrived in the lab room Kalden also looked distracted. Raven couldn't take much comfort in that. Her attention was caught by the test equipment. It was all too familiar, having been the subject of her initial research into the files she'd taken from Kalden's lab. It had formed the most important part of the memory experiments. The same experiments that had left Rachel mind-wiped. As she was strapped to the diagnostic bed, Raven attempted to control her instinctive fear. Rachel had not been an operant Hex. It was this equipment that had triggered her Hex abilities and turned her into Revenge. But Raven was in full possession of all her abilities and she was determined that this equipment shouldn't master her.

As medical nano-probes were attached to her head she allowed herself to sink into the trance-like state she felt when she was using her Hex abilities, but this time she didn't actively try to use them. Instead she observed what the scientists and technicians were doing and waited to see what the effect of the machine would be. When it came, it came like an avalanche. She felt as if her mind was being forcibly opened and streams of data poured in. Door after door, in the innermost recesses of her brain, was being thrown open and searchlights glared in as data flooded her consciousness. Raven fled from the flood of images, retreating through the electronic machinery of the test equipment and back along the power cabling until she had left her body completely and was no longer conscious of what was happening.

Her mind was being systematically shredded. Kalden might call himself a scientist but he had no idea of how to proceed. If this experiment was a success it would turn Raven into a brain-dead zombie, capable of nothing except retaining information, and even that would probably be garbled by the procedure he was using. Raven's fury crested and she knew she would have to return to her body before Kalden destroyed her mind. She was frightened, and furious with herself for her fear. The net stretched before her, shining with a tantalizing light, and she wondered if she could just leave her tormented body behind and sink for ever into its gleaming strands. Then she remembered Kalden and anger achieved dominance over her fear. She brought her thoughts together into a fist and *slammed* back into the test equipment. It halted and juddered at the force of her fury. She tore apart the programming linking the data signals to her body and inserted a new set of operating parameters into the machine. This time it would be set for a wide receive signal and she increased the power accordingly. That much data pumped into her mind could kill her but its effect would be even more devastating on someone without her resources. Using the machine's sensors as an aerial, she turned it back on and poured energy into it. She thought she could hear screaming somewhere in the distance and increased the power further until there was silence again. Only then did she return to her body and open her eyes.

The room looked like a bomb site. All the scientists had collapsed where they were standing, their hands clutched tightly to their heads. Kalden had fallen beside the machine, one hand reaching to turn it off. But he had lost consciousness first and Raven craned her head to look at him. Blood trickled from his nose and he looked as if he was dead.

'Looks' isn't good enough, she told herself and began to struggle with the restraining straps. It took her about five minutes to wriggle out of them. When she did she immediately checked Kalden's prone figure. There was no sign of a pulse.

That was really too kind, she thought to herself. *He deserved it to take longer*.

The two guards who had brought her to the room were also unconscious and, like Kalden, they had no pulse. Stripping the smaller one of his military fatigues, she put them on. The uniform was several sizes too big but it would pass a cursory inspection. She searched both guards quickly for weapons and slung two machine guns and a light pistol from her belt. One of them held the keycard for her cell in his pocket and she took that as well. She also took a slim knife from one of the guards and held it loosely in one hand as she activated the controls to open the door. Outside, the corridor was empty and Raven closed the door again behind her, locking it to prevent immediate discovery of what lay inside. Then she headed down the corridor that led to her cell.

*

Despite his lack of experience, Daniel had been eager to be included in the assault team and there weren't so many volunteers that he had been rejected. So far though he hadn't even loosed off a round from his gun. He had been one of the last to enter the Consulate, under cover of the rolling smoke and, by the time he got inside, the guards on the service door had already been dealt with. He caught a glimpse of Ali Tarrell talking quietly to Avalon, the rock star, and a man with blue hair threaded with gold beads who looked like a ganger. Then his group leader had ordered them forwards and he'd begun this creeping progress though the building, checking carefully around every corner, as they searched for Raven. So far there had only been two outbursts of gunfire. Once when an opening elevator surprised them and the guard inside squeezed off a couple of shots before Jordan dropped him. The second time one of the lead scouts had seen a party approaching from around a corner and opened fire on them. Geraint, their group leader, was carrying a wrist terminal belonging to one of the EF guards and he said there hadn't been a major alert yet. With any luck that meant the EF still didn't know they were in the building. Daniel was relieved. He'd volunteered hoping to be part of the action but now he wasn't so sure it had been a good idea. They'd lost a man in the second firefight and Daniel was well aware that, had he been further forward, that could have been him.

Theirs was only one of three groups searching the building, each assigned separate sections. Every now and again one of the other groups would call in but so far they'd found nothing. The group assigned to the top floors had pulled back, claiming they were certain no prisoners were being held up there and unwilling to start searching offices and alerting people to their presence.

The group Daniel was with was searching the lowest levels and so far they hadn't come across anything more interesting than storage rooms. But the look of the corridors was beginning to change and one of the scouts had been deputized to take out the hidden cameras which were turning up on every corner. Daniel took a firmer grip on his gun and moved forward in the group. He might be afraid but he didn't want to be a coward.

Kez had started when the door opened so soon after the guards taking Raven away. When he recognized the uniformed figure he jumped up in surprise.

'Raven!' he exclaimed and she slapped a hand over his mouth, pointing in annoyance to where they expected the monitors were. Handing him a machine gun, she beckoned him towards the cell door. In seconds they were out and standing in a long corridor, painted in military grey.

'Keep quiet,' she said softly. 'There are hidden cams everywhere and we'll need to take them out. Move carefully.' Then she set off down the corridor and, numb with surprise, Kez followed her.

11
Purge Infected Blood

Sir Charles Alverstead wasn't used to waiting. The demonstrators still hadn't been dispersed, despite him sending out more guards to control them. The EF Consul was away, so he had jurisdiction over the building, but it wasn't helping him solve the problem. The Commander of the Guard still hadn't called him back and Dr Kalden, who had promised him results this morning, was over half an hour late with his report.

That's something I can deal with, Sir Charles thought. The other problems were annoying but this one was downright insulting. He was Kalden's superior in the CPS and the doctor had no right to keep him waiting. He tapped the code for Kalden's lab into the vidcom and waited. There was no answer and he frowned. Tapping in another code, this time one for the security station, he tried again. Again there was no answer and, fuming with anger, he called the Commander of the Guard.

'Commander, why haven't I heard from you earlier?' he demanded. 'And why has the security station been left unmanned?'

'It wasn't left unmanned, sir,' the commander said with a trace of alarm. 'But we had to leave a skeleton staff because most of my men are out dealing with the demonstrators.'

'Then get them back in here,' Alverstead ordered. 'And

check on the prisoners. There's something going on here and I want you to find out what it is!'

Cloud had been watching the demonstration on the news and he had little doubt of what it meant. These were the people Avalon had joined and for some reason they were mounting an attack on the EF Consulate. He thought of Sir Charles Alverstead under siege and smiled slightly. But he didn't take his eyes off the smoke-filled view. Somewhere in that mess Avalon was hiding, he was certain of it. It was no use. The smoke was only getting thicker and it was impossible to make out individual people, let alone who they were. Cloud turned off the vidcom and stood up. For a while he stood motionless in the centre of the room, considering the wisdom of what he was about to do.

'Hell!' he snarled suddenly in the middle of the empty room. 'At least this way I won't feel like a murderer for the rest of my life.'

Making up his mind he headed for his own private flitter and flung himself into the front seat with a feeling of relief. Most of the media people had stopped watching the residence, lured away by the demonstrations. But two flitters took off and started to follow him as he guided his away from the building. He paid them no attention. When he got to his destination they wouldn't be able to follow him any further.

The security station had given Geraint the first clue they were in the right area. It was empty and they fanned out to search for some idea as to where the guards had gone. Daniel was the first to find it, a monitor screen showing a heap of bodies, and he called the others over quickly. Geraint opened a com signal to the other groups.

'Attention all units, attention all units, this is group leader three, we may have found something.'

As confirmation signals came back along the line, Geraint began to describe what they could see on the screen.

'We've found some kind of security control room down here but it's empty. One of the monitors is showing some sort of hospital room. There's a heap of bodies wearing lab coats inside, and two guards. They all look dead.'

'Group leader three, this is Ali,' a voice came back over the link. *'We think you've found the right area and we're coming to join you. Go and find those missing guards. With any luck they'll lead you to Raven.'*

Geraint clicked off the com unit and waved the team out of the room. Their progress was more purposeful now that they knew they were heading in the right direction. Daniel moved up into the leaders, watching for any sign of disturbance ahead.

The corridors were silent but they were watched by the persistent hidden cameras. The leading scouts were becoming adept at spotting them and taking them out. Three corridors on they heard the sound of gunfire and a couple of the leaders started ahead.

'Wait!' Geraint commanded. 'Proceed with extreme caution. Scouts, get on ahead and look out for cameras. We don't know that the room we found is the only security link-up. Everyone else: ready your weapons.'

Daniel inched forward slowly, holding his gun ready but not sure if he'd have the experience to fire it at the right moment. The sound of gunfire stopped and the group moved on cautiously. The scouts ducked back around a corner and waved the rest of the team forward. Geraint went up to join them and they held a whispered conversation. Then Geraint moved to the angle of the corridor and called out:

'Raven!'

'Who's there?' a female voice called back and Daniel glanced at his team-mates. They were all focused on the end of the corridor and Daniel looked back that way as well.

'This is Geraint,' their team leader called. 'We're here to rescue you.'

'Come out then,' the voice called back and Geraint looked at the rest of the team. 'Move slowly,' he told them, 'don't make any sudden movements.' Then he stepped round the angle of the corridor and the rest of the group held their breath. There was no sound and after a few seconds the scouts followed, then the rest of the team.

As Daniel moved after the scouts he found himself in another similar corridor, this one with four dead guards bleeding onto the shining floor. A girl dressed in military fatigues carrying a machine gun stood over the bodies facing Geraint. Beside her a young boy with wide scared eyes held another machine gun pointed at them.

'We're members of Anglecynn,' Geraint explained. 'We're your allies.'

'Glad to hear it,' Raven replied, not lowering her gun.

'If you speak into this com link you'll be able to talk to your friends,' Geraint suggested. 'They're on their way down right now.'

'OK,' Raven agreed and extended her hand.

Geraint tossed the com link across and she caught it easily before switching it on.

'This is Raven,' she said into the speaker. 'Who's there?'

'Raven?' Ali's voice came over the line. *'Raven, are you all right?'*

'Don't ask stupid questions,' Raven said sharply. 'Nice rescue, though. When are you going to get down here so we can leave?'

'We're on our way,' Ali replied. *'But group two reports increased guard activity on the upper levels. Finn thinks we might have difficulty getting out.'*

'Isn't that always the way?' Raven replied. 'See you when you get here.' With that she clicked off the unit and threw it back to Geraint. 'Well, ally,' she said to him, 'we'd better start looking for a way out of here.'

Ali's group was heading for the lower levels of the building when the klaxon started to wail.

'That's torn it,' Luciel muttered and Finn readied his gun ominously.

'Looks like getting out is going to be a hell of a lot harder than getting in,' he said.

'At least we've found Raven,' Avalon said with relief.

'What about Kez?' Luciel asked. 'Is he OK?'

'I didn't think to ask,' Ali blushed. 'But I'm sure Raven would have said if he wasn't.' Luciel looked disappointed and Ali mentally kicked herself for her mistake. But there wasn't time to worry about it now. The wailing alarm might bring guards towards them at any minute. Their team thundered down a set of service stairs, trying to meet up with Raven and group three. Two levels down they heard gunfire and approached slowly until Finn identified Alaric.

'I heard Geraint's located Raven,' he said. 'We were moving to meet up with them when this guard squad charged at us.' He looked over his group with concern and Ali could see several of them were being attended to by team-mates bandaging up bullet wounds. There were two dead bodies on the floor not wearing military uniforms.

'This is getting bloody,' Avalon said and Alaric nodded curtly.

'I think it's time we got out,' he said. 'But it looks like the guards are moving back into the building.'

'Why don't we move on down quickly and meet up with the others?' Ali suggested. 'We'll stand more of a chance together.'

'Agreed,' Alaric replied and Ali was surprised to see people moving instantaneously into position.

The two squads moved on, keeping to a rigid formation with the injured team members in the middle of the group. Ali found herself with Luciel and Alaric at the front while Avalon, Finn and Jeeva brought up the rear. Ten minutes later they encountered one of group three's scouts and were led on to where Geraint, Kez and Raven were waiting. Kez and Luciel greeted each other with relief, exchanging stories quickly while the groups converged. Raven didn't acknowledge anyone in particular but Ali saw her with relief.

'Raven,' she said urgently. 'Do you want to take over? Wraith couldn't come because he was injured so I'm supposed to be in command but . . .'

'Don't be ridiculous,' Raven told her. 'I don't even know who any of these people are. I'm in no state to start taking over.'

'We're Anglecynn,' Alaric explained, overhearing. 'And I'm Alaric.'

Raven nodded to him briskly before asking:

'Do you know what's happened to all the guards?'

'We did have people outside distracting them but now it looks like they're coming back in,' Alaric explained.

'We need to find some kind of way out,' Ali said and to her surprise Raven grinned.

'I can see at least twenty people carrying blasters,' she said. 'Twenty blasters can make their own way out.'

'Good idea,' Alaric agreed. 'Someone find an exterior wall.'

'I'll do it!' Jordan said, speaking up for the first time. Alaric winced slightly but didn't try to prevent her.

'Take someone with you,' he ordered and Daniel stepped forward instantly.

'I'll go with Jordan,' he said. 'I know this building a little.'

'Get to it then,' Geraint told them and they both took off instantly.

Ali looked after them. She recognized Daniel and admired him for stepping forward. She found herself hoping that he hadn't seen her try to hand command over to Raven. This was probably the only opportunity she'd ever have to look as if she was important.

'I'd better contact the people outside and find out what's going on,' Alaric said. 'Watch my back.'

The people nearest to him readied their guns as Alaric flipped open his communicator and entered the com code of the protest coordinator.

'This is Alaric,' he said. 'What's up out there.'

'It's like a war zone,' Carl's voice came back. *'There are thousands of Seccies out here and we're running out of gas. I don't know how much longer we can hold them.'*

'What about the EF guards?'

'Most of them are heading back inside but it's hard to tell how many are left,' Carl replied. *'The Seccies have been shooting pretty indiscriminately and I reckon they got quite a few of the EF people as well as some of the media snoops.'*

'The Seccies shot media people?' Alaric asked incredulously.

'Looks like quite a few,' Carl replied. *'And they don't look happy about it. More of them have turned up than were here this morning and they're filming the whole thing.'*

'Useful to know,' Alaric replied. 'Thanks, Carl. You can pull back soon now but I want you to hold the flitters ready. We'll be coming out the side of the building and we'll need collecting if you can.'

'We'll do our best,' Carl replied. *'Don't take too long.'* Then the line went dead and Alaric holstered the com unit. As he did so Geraint's unit chimed.

'Geraint,' he said, answering it.

'Jordan here,' came the reply. *'We've found an exterior wall. West of your position but we'll have to come back and show you the way.'*

'Good work,' Geraint replied. 'Get back here as quickly as you can.' He turned off the unit and looked at the rest of them. 'Looks like we're moving,' he said.

Cloud's flitter streaked past the final bridge and swung down in an elegant curve towards the thick blue smoke. It wasn't as enveloping as it had been on the news earlier. A troop of Seccie police with riot shields and gas masks were advancing on the protesters, opening fire on the flitters in which the demonstrators hid. Cloud watched the confusion, circling round the building to lose his media escort. On the second circuit he ducked his flitter down below the smoke and waited. Three seconds later the media flitters swung past above him and he smiled to himself, moving the little craft slowly forward while keeping out of range of the shooting Seccies.

From his vantage point he was ideally placed to see what happened next. The last of the protesters reached their flitters and they started taking off, still belching blue smoke down on the Seccies. Then, as the Seccies were firing on the flitters, not making any attempt to distinguish between those belonging to the demonstrators and those with media slogans, the side of the building exploded. Half a level of the EF Consulate opened up as its exterior wall fell open and debris showered on the crowds below. Half the Seccies turned to fire on the building just as a troop of EF guards ran out of the main doors with the same intention. The two groups opened fire on each other as the rest of the Seccies shot at the flitters.

The demonstrators were taking advantage of the opportunity to skim their flitters up to the side of the building, risking the ricocheting shots as they helped people on board. Cloud watched as about half the people from the Consulate were pulled to safety and the flitters that rescued them took off. It was then that he saw the distinctive swirl of red hair he'd been looking for. He didn't know what Avalon was doing halfway up the side of the EF building but he intended to find out and he edged the little flitter upwards, trying to stay out of sight of the Seccies and the EF guards. He was wise to do so because the confusion was being sorted out below. Although about half the forces on the level were still shooting each other, taking revenge for the deaths of their fellow officers, the others had identified the real enemy and were blasting the flitters as the demonstrators tried to pull their friends to safety.

It wasn't going to work. Cloud could see the flitters being hit and gradually they pulled off, taking the people they already had on board to safety. Five people remained standing in the blast area, firing back at the Seccies as the last remaining flitter hovered, waiting to take them to safety. One person managed to get on and Cloud recognized her as the blond girl who had been in the residence. Then the flitter was hit by a direct shot and tumbled almost the entire level before stabilizing. It swung around as if its pilot intended to return but then circled back in another direction, leaving the scene. Avalon and her companions backed away from the ledge, heading back into the building.

Cloud's hands were on the flitter's controls before he realized what he was doing. If Avalon went back into the building she was almost certain to be captured or killed by the EF guards. Even if she found another way out, more Seccies were arriving all the time. Cloud's flitter hurtled up through the dispersing smoke and headed directly for the side of the building. He heard blaster shots sizzling past him and then felt the flitter lurch as one hit the small craft. Forcing the vehicle to greater acceleration he hurtled up the side of the building and through the hole the terrorists had made in its side. The corridor on the other side of the hole was narrow and he pulled back on the controls, forcing the flitter to slow its progress as it shot between the walls, a finger's breadth away from them. It came to a halt just before the next turning and Cloud hit the door release. As he exited the flitter he came face to face with four figures, standing astonished at the end of the corridor.

Avalon stared as the flitter rushed towards her, blackening the walls of the passageway with the heat of its passing. When the door opened and Cloud stepped out she was literally speechless with surprise. Finn and Geraint didn't have the same problem.

'My God!' Geraint exclaimed, awestruck by the sight.

'Freakin' insanity,' the ganger murmured behind him. 'Who's this schizo?'

'Cloud Estavisti,' Raven informed them, already heading towards the flitter. 'How fortunate. I was beginning to doubt the success of this rescue.'

'Cloud's not part of the mission,' Avalon warned, finding her voice at last. 'He tried to betray us to the CPS. He's probably here to do it again.'

Cloud's dark blue eyes met hers with an unreadable expression then he turned to Raven.

'I am here to help you,' he told her. 'Despite what may have happened in the past. And you don't exactly have a lot of options.'

'Succinctly put,' Raven acknowledged. 'Everyone get in the flitter.'

Avalon hesitated for a second but, as Raven had already admitted, she couldn't think of an alternative. Finn and Geraint climbed in beside her but Raven continued to face Cloud.

'I'll drive,' she informed him. The dancer looked as if he was about to protest then he shrugged and stepped aside, allowing Raven to take the pilot's seat as he crossed to the other side of the craft and took the seat next to her.

Raven touched the controls and the doors hissed shut.

'How are you going to get this thing out again?' Finn asked cynically. 'There's no room to turn.'

'Then I won't turn,' Raven replied and her fingers sped across the controls in a blur of movement. As they did so, the flitter took off. Hurtling backwards through the cramped corridor, charring the walls once more as it passed by, the flitter shot out of the building without even grazing the sides. A fusillade of shots exploded around them but Raven was still backing off and the flitter streaked past the rain of blaster fire before coming about in a tight turn and shooting for the sky.

By the time the sounds of pursuit began behind them, Raven was already five levels up and still accelerating.

'Where are we going?' Avalon asked in bewilderment as the young Hex guided their craft further upwards.

'Gangland,' Raven replied curtly, her fingers still flying over the control board.

'Down is the other direction,' Cloud said diffidently and Raven flashed him a smile.

'Just a diversion,' she said, still smiling. 'Seccies never have any sense of perspective.'

'Perspective?' Geraint said quietly, looking at Avalon.

The megastar shrugged and then blinked as a wash of sunlight fell across her face.

The flitter shot out of the city heights, sailing up into the cold winter sky. Below them they could see the tops of the skyscrapers, reaching up towards the clouds. Then Raven pulled the flitter around in a dizzying turn and they circled around the city. The towers were immense; it was impossible to see their entire height from any one point, but at the edges of the city some of them were shorter, still beginning their course towards the sky. Raven guided the flitter towards these stunted giants and once more the darkness of the city enclosed them. Once more they were in the depths of London, heading towards the ganglands.

'No sense of perspective,' Raven repeated. 'They saw us go up, so they go up. It'll be at least a week before they realize they've lost us.'

Wraith paced anxiously across the floor of the control room. He'd been watching the events at the EF Consulate unfold on the news. The government had attempted to impose a news blackout when they realized what was happening but for once the media networks had resisted. Five reporters had died during the firefight, all of them felled by Seccie or EF weapons, and the news networks were in no mood to censor the story.

As a result Wraith had watched as the side of the building exploded and the demonstrators had attempted to haul the rescue party to safety. He had scrutinized the images for any sign of Raven but he hadn't seen her until the last flitter had pulled away, leaving four pathetic figures marooned. He cursed Raven for remaining behind while the people who had come to rescue her left and was within an inch of running for a flitter himself, however late he was bound to arrive. It was then that the luxury flitter had streaked up the side of the Consulate and into the gaping hole in the building's side. By the time it reappeared the newsfeeds had identified it as belonging to Cloud and were speculating excitedly on what this might mean. A news anchor began to explain their current theory.

'It's a dramatic ending to the story of Avalon's disappearance but now the answer seems clear. This is a picture of Avalon, left behind after the attack on the EF building that has been raging for the past three hours. Now Cloud Estavisti, who has refused to talk to the media about the reason for the megastar's disappearance, has appeared as well. Two of the members of Europe's leading rock band appear to have joined an underground terrorist group known as Anglecynn. We can only speculate on the reasons why, since it doesn't look like they'll be giving any press conferences any time soon.'

A picture was flashed up of the four people who'd been left behind and the anchor added:

'As to who these other people are, again we can only guess. We don't even know the reason Anglecynn attacked the EF Consulate today. But the multiple fatalities we have seen today did not come at their hands.

While we don't know the reason for its attack we can see its results. Vidcam images broadcast earlier have shown that the protesters were unarmed, even if their counterparts inside the building were not. They attempted to hold off the combined might of the EF and the Security Services with peaceful means and many of their number were brutally shot down as were those five brave reporters who attempted to bring you the truth of these events.'

Wraith was curious to see what the media would say next but the anchor's speech was interrupted by another live broadcast of the events unfolding at the Consulate. Wraith watched as Cloud's flitter flew out of the building backwards, curved around and disappeared from view. As he watched, his body relaxed from its state of tension. There was only one person who drove like that.

12
A General Eclipse

The flitter came to rest inside the gangland fortress and Wraith ran to meet it. As the doors opened and Raven appeared he swept her into a one-armed hug. For a change Raven didn't resist his spontaneous show of affection but after a few moments she stepped away and he released her.

'I thought we'd lost you,' he said quietly and Raven looked at him gravely.

'I wasn't sure myself,' she admitted. Then she grinned. 'Looks like we've caused a lot of trouble,' she said. 'The government won't find it so easy to cover this up.'

'That's true,' Wraith agreed. Then, remembering something, he turned to Cloud. 'I don't know how to thank you,' he said simply. 'But it looks like I'll have time to find a way. You were recognized by the media.'

'I was expecting that,' Cloud replied, looking unfazed by the thought. 'It's not a problem as long as you're prepared to take me in.'

Avalon looked anxious and spoke pleadingly to Wraith.

'Cloud's made up for his betrayal, hasn't he?'

'As far as I'm concerned, he has,' Wraith agreed and looked at Raven for confirmation.

'He can stay,' she said with a shrug. 'One more

megastar doesn't make a lot of difference – it's the fifty terrorists who surprised me.'

'Anglecynn!' Geraint exclaimed. 'We have to contact them! We don't know how badly the Seccies hit them.'

'I'll contact them immediately,' Wraith agreed, leading the way to the control room.

Kez had been one of the first to be lifted off and he watched the arrival of the other flitters anxiously. Although there were mercifully few dead, many of the Anglecynn members had been badly injured during the Seccie attacks and, as the flitters unloaded their passengers at Dragon's Nest, the administrative staff hurried to give them medical attention. In the confusion, Kez searched for his friends among the wounded and their helpers. He found Ali talking to Daniel Hammond as he was being treated for blaster wounds. To Kez's surprise Ali smiled when she saw him.

'I'm glad you're all right,' she told him. 'It wasn't the same without you and Raven.'

'Have you seen Raven?' Kez asked anxiously. 'I can't find her anywhere.'

'No.' Ali's eyes darkened. 'I hope she made it off. Things got kind of crazy at the end.'

'I'll keep looking,' Kez said quickly, already turning away.

'Tell us when you find her,' Ali called after him but Kez was already gone.

He hurried through the ranks of people, asking everyone if they'd seen Raven and getting increasingly panicked when no one had. Luciel and Jeeva had arrived on one of the later flitters and had only been able to tell him that Ali, Raven and Finn, as well as some of the Anglecynn members, had still been in the building when they left. Finally he came to a halt. No more flitters were arriving and he'd spoken to everyone in the room. The grim certainty that Raven hadn't made it was beginning to sink in when Alaric strode into the room.

The terrorist leader's clothes bore blaster burns and he was bleeding from a cut on his head but he had evidently considered his injuries too light to attend to at once. Now he called for Anglecynn's attention and everyone turned to look at him, save for the medical workers who were still attending to the injured.

'I've just had a call from Wraith,' he announced. 'It seems Cloud Estavisti turned up to lift out the last people from the building. They're all all right.'

'Does that include Raven?' Kez asked quickly and Alaric nodded.

'Raven, Geraint, Avalon and Finn,' he said. Then he looked around at the assembled company. 'I'd like to thank everyone for the part they played in today's operation,' he said. 'I know no one expected to have to engage in a mission of that nature on such short notice. But your work today almost certainly saved the life of someone who may help to save many more. Together we grieve for our dead but I'm grateful the casualties were not more heavy. No one, especially myself, expected that the Seccie response would not only be so violent but so undisciplined.

'Everyone will need to be debriefed and I'll arrange a meeting with the Hex group as soon as is feasible. But for now I'll leave you to have your injuries attended to and to get some sleep. However, those who are not wounded will be called upon for the usual watches and everyone should be aware of the possibility of Seccie reprisals. I don't believe that anyone was followed here but I'd like you to remain cautious just in case.'

With that he finished speaking and a murmur of conversation resumed. Alaric crossed to where Kez was standing.

'Wraith is sending a flitter to collect you,' he said. 'And Ali, Luciel and someone called Jeeva.'

'Thank you,' Kez said and looked at the terrorist leader with genuine gratitude. 'For everything.'

Alaric smiled at him then looked over at the injured people.

'I must go,' he said. 'Please remind Wraith I would like to meet with all your group as soon as possible.'

'I will,' Kez promised and Alaric hurried back to his people.

Although Wraith urged Raven to sleep she refused to rest until she'd looked over the new base and especially the control room. Since she insisted, Avalon and Wraith accompanied her, with Cloud diffidently following. Finn left to collect the other members of the group with strict instructions to be careful not to lead any Seccies near the Anglecynn base. Raven inspected everything, including the unused rooms which Wraith hadn't discovered a purpose for yet. She raised her eyebrows at Ali's blue-green scheme of decoration in the apartment section but looked relieved when they eventually entered the control room.

'The Countess sent over two technicians to put everything together,' Avalon told her. 'Since then we've been trying to understand how it all works.'

'You've done reasonably well,' Raven replied, running her fingers over the central terminals. 'Although I'll have to install a security system before someone trashes the entire computer network.' She turned away from the terminal and rubbed her forehead briefly.

'You look tired,' Wraith said sympathetically. 'You've

seen everything now – go and sleep for a while. We can talk when the others get back.'

'All right,' Raven agreed, with an uncharacteristic submission. 'We'll talk later.' With that she headed off to the apartment area, leaving them in the control room.

Cloud watched her leave, then turned to speak to Wraith.

'Perhaps there's somewhere I could wait, as well,' he suggested. 'Since there are doubtless matters you would like to discuss in my absence.'

Wraith and Avalon exchanged a glance. Neither of them was prepared to deny that they would have to discuss Cloud's admission to the group in greater detail. But equally they didn't want to seem ungrateful for his involvement.

'Why don't you wait in the apartment suite, then,' Avalon said finally. 'We could just relax and watch the vidscreen for a while.'

Raven slept deeply without dreaming. She didn't even wake up when Finn returned with the others and they gathered in the apartment's living room to exchange stories. She slept through their discussion of Cloud's role in the group and the decision to give him a chance as one of them. She eventually awoke late the next day when the building was mostly silent.

Emerging from the room she had claimed as hers, Raven wandered through the building. Wraith and Avalon she found in the control room and the vidscreens showed her Luciel and Kez dismantling a flitter in the vehicle bay and Jeeva giving Ali and Cloud a shooting lesson in the main hall.

'You found a good place,' Wraith commented and she smiled slightly.

'For now,' Raven agreed. 'But I imagine things will change.'

'The story's still all over the media,' Avalon told her. 'There hasn't been an official statement yet though.'

'Probably still trying to decide how to cover everything up,' Raven replied. 'But it won't be easy. The Seccies have been out of control ever since this initiative to wipe out the Hexes came in and I doubt it's going to get better. Not after what the CPS learned from me.'

'What did they learn?' Wraith asked quietly. 'I hoped that they wouldn't experiment on you immediately.'

'A forlorn hope,' Raven told him. 'They started testing me almost immediately but they didn't learn anything from that. What the CPS have discovered is that a solitary Hex is capable of neutralizing the best resources they have. I killed Kalden and most of his scientists. It will be a while before they can duplicate his work and now that work has proved useless against me they may not want to.' She looked thoughtful. 'I suspect the CPS might now decide to adopt a more drastic solution.'

'More drastic how?' Avalon asked and Raven shrugged.

'We'll have to see,' she said. 'But I think, in the circumstances, I might need to start teaching the rest of you sooner rather than later.'

'I agree,' Wraith added. 'What happened yesterday is bound to have an affect. Anglecynn are certainly worried about that.'

'Yes, our terrorist allies,' Raven said. 'I still don't exactly know how they come into all this.'

'Neither do they,' Wraith told her. 'That still has to be decided. They helped with the rescue attempt because they were persuaded that the extermination laws are wrong. But after that I don't know how much support they'll want to give us or how much we should give them.'

'Alaric wants to meet with us tonight,' Avalon told her. 'He seems to be their leader and he's anxious to gain an advantage for Anglecynn through working with us.'

'I've no objection,' Raven replied. She glanced at the vidscreen where Ali and Cloud were firing rounds at a battered target, hitting it about one shot in ten. 'They might be terrorists but at least they can shoot straight.'

'Is that going to be important?' Avalon asked carefully. 'So far your group has tried to avoid violence.'

'I designed this place with self-defence in mind,' Raven told her. 'It's intended to be a fortress. The Seccies and the CPS aren't going to go away and the European Federation surely sees us as a threat. In the circumstances, some kind of martial expertise would be useful and Anglecynn seem to have that.'

'We'll talk to them about it this evening,' Wraith agreed. 'Maybe by then there'll be some more news.'

Sir Charles Alverstead wasn't eager to release anything to the media. He met with Adam Hammond and the Prime Minister, George Chesterton, at the Houses of Parliament. The EF building was still a wreck after the terrorist attack and had been closed down until the EF Special Forces had arrived to determine what had gone wrong. Alverstead had a feeling that he might lose his job over this, although he hoped he might be able to blame the whole fiasco on Kalden. The doctor was dead as a result of his underestimation of Raven, and his experimentation might have to die with him. In the meantime Alverstead's priority was saving his own skin and that necessitated a media cover-up.

'The media aren't being very cooperative,' the Security Minister was explaining. 'In fact they've been flooding my department with demands and complaints. They claim that the Security Services used unreasonable force on the demonstrators and they're threatening to sue because of the media deaths.'

'Can't you find some way to blame that on the Hexes?' the Prime Minister asked. 'The last thing this country needs is a scandal in the Security Services.'

'Perhaps the last thing this country needs is a media that cannot be controlled,' Alverstead suggested. 'The EF has already discussed bringing in stronger regulatory measures. Perhaps they could be brought forward.'

'Good idea,' Chesterton agreed. 'The Federation Council will back us up if necessary, I'm sure. I only hope they don't blame us for allowing this Hex threat to occur in this country.'

'At least the media have helped us in one area,' Adam Hammond told him. 'We now have reliable vid images of the Hex named Raven. We should be able to trace her background with that.'

'All the same, they need to be brought under control,' Chesterton said. 'Inform the controllers of the newsfeeds that they will be expected to comply with Federation law and issue a gag order on all reports concerning the Hex problem other than official statements. Let's not give these terrorists a platform to address the world.'

The Hexes and Anglecynn met by mutual consent at Dragon's Nest. Avalon had volunteered to remain behind to guard the Fortress but Wraith had insisted that they all be there. Finn and Jeeva, who had returned to working for the Countess, had been hired instead to watch the control room. As Alaric's people issued them permission to approach, Wraith looked around the group with satisfaction. Raven was still looking weary but there seemed to be no lasting effects from the experimentation. Ali and Luciel were both looking more confident and Kez was more talkative, sharing their conversation without looking intimidated by Ali. Cloud Estavisti was still a mystery. He talked quietly to Avalon but Wraith couldn't make out their conversation. Raven seemed to guess the direction of his thoughts as they coasted through the depths of the city towards Anglecynn's base.

'I think it will work out,' she said. 'It could even be fun.'

'I'm not sure I want to be responsible for so many people,' Wraith said quietly.

'Then don't be.' Raven shrugged and lay back in her seat. 'Let them be responsible for themselves. Everyone's here because they chose to be, after all.'

'Even you?' Wraith asked. 'I recall you said forming a solidarity group was a waste of time.'

'I'm here for the time being,' Raven told him. 'And I've been revising my opinion a little. Let's just see what happens.'

The members of Anglecynn were waiting for them in their main common room and Alaric greeted the Hex group with a smile.

'I'm impressed by your base,' Raven told him. 'The depths of the city are generally considered uninhabitable.'

'It's something we take advantage of,' Alaric replied. 'But it makes expansion difficult. We can only hide so many people here.'

'You seem to have done well,' Wraith said. 'The Seccies must be furious you've evaded them for so long.'

'We might not be able to evade them much longer,' Alaric said grimly. 'We have sources in the city who sometimes pass us information. Word is the government is going to use the events at the Consulate as an excuse to introduce more EF controls. Our fight just got a lot harder.'

'Maybe not necessarily,' Raven told him. 'I'm getting tired of the way the CPS is hunting me. If your group is prepared to support us there are things we'd be willing to give you in return.'

'We've discussed this amongst ourselves already,' Geraint said, speaking up for the first time. 'Most of us feel your cause is something we can commit to but we still don't know exactly what you can offer in return.'

'How does complete control of the net sound to you?' Raven asked and the Anglecynn members exchanged glances.

'Is that something you can do?' Alaric asked, looking doubtful.

'Not quite yet,' Raven told him. She turned to glance at Avalon, Ali and Luciel. 'But yes, I think it's possible and it's something I intend to work towards. I think it's time that Hexes made things difficult for the CPS and I can teach any Hex how to use the net, although it will be a while before they can use it as well as I can.' She didn't say there was a possibility that it might never occur. She still didn't know how unusual her own abilities were and, although the other members of the group might not be able to emulate her, she hadn't discounted the chance of finding new Hexes who could.

'Is that something we're prepared to work for?' Alaric asked, turning to address the whole of Anglecynn. Heads nodded across the room. Even those who were still uneasy about working with the Hexes were swayed by the prospect of control of the net. The agreement seemed, for the moment, to be unanimous. 'It looks like we're with you,' Alaric told Raven.

'You've already assisted us immensely,' Wraith told him. 'I'm sure none of us will regret the decision.'

'At the moment we need all the allies we can get,' Geraint said seriously. 'The EF is getting stronger all the time. If we can't move against them soon, we may never be able to.'

For a while the room was silent as everyone present considered the possibility. Raven was the first to speak.

'They have more to be afraid of than we do,' she said. 'We know what they're capable of. But they don't have the slightest idea what we can do to them.'

The Federation Council buildings at Versailles were as imposing as the ancient palace which still formed a small part of them. The glittering towers and battlements now hid an array of twenty-fourth century weaponry and the centre of the EF dominated Europe as the French kings had once controlled France. The Council's word was law across the states that fell under its protection. Although there were occasional problems when groups attempted to shake off the yoke of the Federation these seldom caused the Council any real concern.

Now a new threat had developed. The Hex problem, supposedly contained centuries previously, had broken out anew in an alarming fashion. It had been years since a rogue Hex had survived to adulthood to trouble the EF with their presence, although such threats had occasionally occurred. Now another mutant had escaped and destroyed not only the secret experimentation programme, known only to the governments of Europe, but also the balance of power of the British Government. Britain had been one of the last member nations to come under EF control. The Federation had not yet imposed the full force of its dominance. The Hex threat meant that things would have to change and the British Prime Minister had accepted that EF control was the only choice to combat a possible rebellion.

In other EF-controlled countries the CPS had worked effectively with the local peacekeeping forces to eradicate the Hex threat. In Britain this policy had obviously failed. Now it was time for a new approach. With Federation troops stationed in Britain, upholding the government and supporting the CPS, there would be nowhere for the Hexes to hide. The rebellion could be crushed and this latest mutant leader eradicated. Within the jewel-covered might of the Federation Council buildings, plans were being set in motion to strike against the threat they only knew by the name of Raven.

Rhiannon Lassiter
HEX: GHOSTS

In the depths of the city, a new force is stirring.

HEX

They leave no trace as their minds fly free and silent
through the computer system

HEX

They are the ghosts – Hexes who should have
been exterminated long ago.
The government wanted them dead.
The world was not ready for them.
But now they are going to make people listen.

HEX

This is the future . . .

The exhilarating final blast of the Hex trilogy.
1. Hex 2. Hex: Shadows 3. Hex: Ghosts

John Marsden
LETTERS FROM THE INSIDE

Dear Tracey
I don't know why I'm answering your ad, to be honest. It's not like I'm into pen pals, but it's a boring Sunday here, wet, everyone's out, and I thought it'd be something different . . .

Dear Mandy
Thanks for writing. You write so well, much better than me, I put the ad in for a joke, like a dare, and yours was the only good answer . . .

Two girls begin a friendship – two strangers exchanging letters, getting to know each other a little better every time they write.

Sometimes writing's easier than talking. Secrets and fears seem safer on paper. And both girls have plenty of each – fears they hardly dare to confront; secrets that could blow their lives apart . . .

'John Marsden's *Letters from the Inside* is, in a word, unforgettable. But this epistolary novel deserves more than one word. It is absolutely shattering as it brings to vivid life two teenage girls and then strangles your heart over what happens to their relationship . . . John Marsden is a major writer who deserves world-wide acclaim.'
Robert Cormier

Caroline B. Cooney
BURNING UP

Macey has been living in the same town all her life.
She's fifteen. Everything was easy.
Not any more.

A secret from the past is about to explode into her life. A secret no one will discuss. Forty years ago there was a fire across the road from her grandparents. A fire which never quite died down. And a man was driven out of town never to return.

The stench of smoke is everywhere.
Someone has set Macey's world on fire.
Does she really want to know the truth?

Celia Rees
TRUTH OR DARE

A room of secrets in a house of lies . . .

When Josh explores his grandmother's house he finds an attic up a closed-off staircase. In it is a collection of strange drawings by his uncle, Patrick, who died suddenly in his teens. But he has no grave, and his name is never spoken.

And Josh begins to uncover the dark truth his family has hidden for forty years . . .

'*Truth or Dare* doesn't let up – and hits you with a final twist.'
Daily Telegraph

'An unsettling, unputdownable mystery.'
TES

'A compelling story in which the secrecy and shame of the past are shed to reveal a rather wonderful and utterly contemporary present.'
The Scotsman

'A moving book.'
The Times

'Celia Rees recounts a terrible human tragedy.'
Children's Book of the Week, The Guardian